I0699674

Different Vessels

Different Vessels

Jonathan Lee

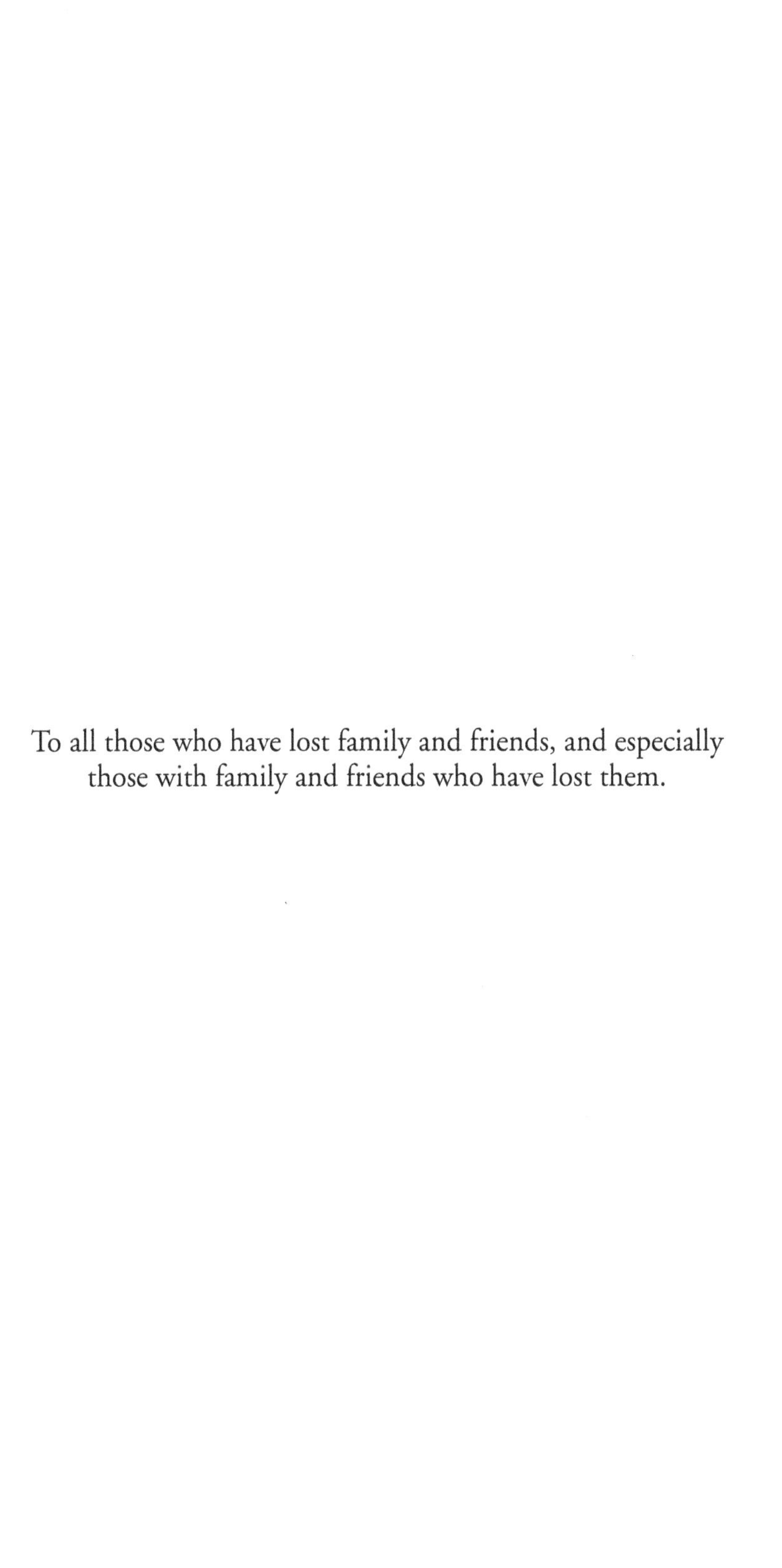

To all those who have lost family and friends, and especially
those with family and friends who have lost them.

HE awoke to the faint sound of a distant alarm. A low, brash tone repeated incessantly like a nagging buzz saw urging him to get up. He didn't know where he was, yet it seemed familiar. There were times in the past when he had awoken in a strange place, only to quickly recall he was on vacation or staying over at someone else's place. Of course, now, he suddenly realized he couldn't actually remember any of those times. He couldn't remember much at all…

The man felt the fog of time around him—not unlike this dark smoky interior in which he found himself. His life had faded away like a dream, it would seem, and now all he had left was the present. A black space of indeterminate size, filled with little lights. Whites and reds and greens, twinkling like Christmas lights in the dark.

When that irritating alarm would sound, the deep black of his surroundings was interrupted by a dull red from some distant light source. Whenever that faint red would flash, he could make out rolling clouds of thin smoke billowing through the inky interior. Farther away, he could make out a whole shaft of light, like the crack in the ceiling of a cave.

Suddenly his senses were assaulted by some sharp smell. Plastic. He didn't know the first time he had learned that association, but he knew it well now. The fire must have been eating away at the plastic sheaths of the electric wires inside the panels of the ship—if not the panels themselves.

Ship? Yes, a spaceship. He still didn't know where he was or what turn of events had led to his current predicament, but he understood now the nature of the situation. The ship was on fire, and he had to get out.

He clumsily arose to his feet and struggled to regain his balance after rising gave him a sudden woozy feeling. He instinctively put his hand to the side of his head, which was now throbbing with a dull pain. As he did, he felt a warm wetness. Blood.

He stumbled through the dark, and made his way toward the light. As he stepped forth into that glowing column of luminescence, he was suddenly blinded. His eyelids reacted immediately and clenched tight. Even then, it was still too much, and he instinctively raised his hands to his eyes for more shielding.

After a moment, he lowered his hands. He then slowly opened his eyes, letting them adjust to the burning brightness. As he did, he saw before him a ladder. That ladder looked to reached up from his present gloom into the heavens, for as he cast his eyes above he could see now the bright blue sky. It was a long way up.

Left step. Grab. Lift. Right step. Grab. Lift. Breathe. He ascended this way up the metal rungs, making his slow escape from the dark smoky inferno below towards that patch of bright blue heaven above. His ascension was filled with struggle and pain. His head pounded with every beat of his heart, and his weary limbs ached and burned with every climb.

About halfway up, he suddenly was struck by sudden doubt. Was he even going the right way? How would he get down from the top of the ship? He didn't even know the ship's shape. Only the vague awareness of a giant wedge-like form with rounded wings. The thought was like a half-remembered dream. He didn't know if it could be trusted.

He shook his head and carried on. There was only one way out he could see when he was down in the gloom, so what other choice did he have? Once he got to the top, he could always go back down… assuming there was still time.

As he ascended, he passed by floors of devastation. Hanging wires. Scattered debris. Whirring and crackling sounds in the dark. The distant moan of creaking metal. And every ruined floor was bathed in that oscillating red light and the grating sound of alert that accompanied it.

In the midst of that regular nagging noise, he heard something different. A faint organic sound like a murmur. A voice? He stopped and waited. His lungs insisted he catch his breath, but he tried to use his nose alone, tried to tuck his lower lip and direct his breath away from his ears, anything he could to listen. And he listened for some time, before he finally heard it again.

It was definitely a voice.

"Hello…?" he called out to the dark.

A moment passed and no reply, as he gazed into the void.

"Tyler?" the voice finally returned.

The reply shook him like thunder, and lightning traveled up his spine in turn. So he was not alone. It only made sense. Yet for some strange reason he wasn't expecting it.

Tyler? Was that his name? He couldn't mistake the tone in that voice. That subtle lilt upward that told him that single word was a question. How would he answer it? The only honest reply would be "I don't know," and that suddenly struck him with embarrassment. An adult man should at least know his own name. Yet another one of those little facts he managed to recall.

Before he could respond, the voice continued: "I guess it makes sense that *you* would survive, you son of a bitch. Only the *good* die young…"

The gruff man out there in the shadows certainly seemed to be certain he had the right man. Tyler guessed "Tyler" was as good a name as any. Although apparently the same could not be said about the man attached to that name.

Was the gruff voice teasing him? Was this an old friend? No… the bitterness and outright malice in the voice was unmistakably there.

Tyler's eyes darted back and forth as he quickly processed the present situation. He didn't know who this disembodied voice was. He didn't even know who *he* was—apart from a name and an unfavorable opinion. Nevertheless, he could hear pain in that voice. Its coughs and groans echoed in the murk. Whoever this man was, he likely needed help. But was there enough time…?

"Do you know how much time we have to get out of here?" Tyler called out.

"We…?" the man replied. The bitterness from before was replaced with genuine confusion.

"Yes. I mean to come get you…" Tyler replied. He immediately gulped, attempting to swallow down his fear.

What came next filled Tyler with confusion of his own.

Out of the black, in between the buzz of the alarm, came laughter. Uproarious laughter. The gruff man was cackling with genuine delight. Tyler smirked nervously, feeling like he had missed out on the joke. The deep roaring cackles were cut short by a cough. Violent coughing that betrayed the man's perilous condition.

"Where are you?" Tyler asked with concern as he stepped forward into the inky interior.

"Looking to play hero now, eh?" the man called out. And there was the bitterness again.

Tyler couldn't help but get a little irritated at the man's remark. "Would you please just tell me where you are?"

"Heh…" the voice snorted with amusement. After a few beats, it continued, "Alright, johnny boy. Not sure what game you're playing at this time, but I've got nothing better to—" His condescending remarks were cut short by a series of coughs.

Tyler picked up his pace, moving in the voice's direction. He trod carefully, using what little illumination the red flash offered to make his way across the debris-laden floor. Tyler started to question why he was doing this. The man offered nothing to him but disdain. He wasn't sure what "johnny boy" was supposed to mean, but he took it as an insult. Did he really deserve this kind of treatment? Of course, maybe he did. And Tyler was disturbed at the thought.

After a slow, tedious trek through a landscape of destruction, and a bit of awkward conversation, Tyler caught a glimpse of the grizzled man's shadow. There was a faint whirring hum, interrupted by occasional sizzles and pops as sparks flashed in the dark. In those brief bright flashes, Tyler could see more hanging wires, and a mess of debris covering the man from the waist down.

"Do you know what has you trapped?" Tyler asked.

"Probably an engineering panel. Pretty sure it crushed my whole damn leg. Good thing I found this…" the man replied and tapped something. It was a box or case of something Tyler could dimly make out in the gloom between the little flashes of electrical sparks.

"If I lift it up enough, do you think you'll be able to pull your leg out from under it?"

"It's worth a try…"

The tone in the man's voice had progressively changed. The sharp edge had disappeared, along with the bitterness, and he had become more congenial. He was still puzzled more than ever, but at this point it was obvious that—for whatever reason—Tyler genuinely meant to help.

Tyler felt along the smooth surface in the dark, finally finding the bottom and gripping it tightly. The old stranger fiddled with something in his hand, before a broad, bright beam flashed forth from the old man's fist. Tyler paused at the shock of the flash before letting his eyes adjust to the new light.

He wasted no time to survey his surroundings, but instead immediately continued with the task at hand. And it was not a small one. The panel was as tall and wide as a man, and it weighed at least as much as well. Tyler strained with all his strength to push the panel away.

With a great thud, it came crashing down. And Tyler soon after collapsed to the floor, panting from the exertion. After taking a moment to catch his breath, he let his eyes glide over to the lighted space extending away from the old man.

Tyler blinked a bit and gulped at the sight. Blood and bone like scattered debris littered two badly mangled legs. His eyes drifted up to the face of the grizzled old man, who sat still and slightly slack jawed with wide eyes in the dark.

"Shit…" the old man finally remarked.

"Are you—I mean… are we… what do we do?" Tyler replied.

"We?"

"Well, how are we getting out here if you can't… I mean… you can't walk."

"Ya think?" the old man replied with the bitterest of sarcasm, as he rolled his eyes and let out a sigh and a groan.

Tyler decided it best to keep his mouth shut. And so he ran his fingers through his hair, let out a sigh of his own, rubbed his eyes a bit, and all the other little things men do when they're overwhelmed and lost. And so Tyler and the old man sat together in the dark a bit, quietly. He stared listlessly into the field of light beyond, while the old man chewed on his lower lip and rubbed his neck in uneasy contemplation.

After a moment, the old man spoke. "We need to get a good idea of where we're at with the ship. I heard the fire suppression systems kick in a bit ago, but our communications are down, as is the on-board diagnostics network. So if you can get out and use the polyscan and show me the readings, I can…"

A sudden creak and rumble distracted Tyler's attention. He peered off into the dark with concern. The shudder of the floor sent a shiver down his spine.

"Hey, are you listening, asshole?" the cranky codger asked with obvious irritation.

"What? Uh, yes, yes. Wha-what do you need me to do exactly?"

The old man replied with a sigh and an eye roll, and reached for a nearby box of some kind. In response to the quick tap of the man's finger, the box lit up. It was a device of some sort which painted the old man's face blue with a faint light dimly shining from its front surface. Tyler came around to peer down at the device, which he now saw had a screen.

Over the course of a quarter-hour or so, the grizzled crank showed Tyler how to operate the polyscan, like an impatient young grandfather showing a teenager how to make a pot of coffee. Although his instructor was condescending and rude, Tyler nodded along and listened closely as the old man pointed to configuration settings, operational modes, and on-screen graphs of various kinds.

Just as they discussed, Tyler made his way back through the wreckage to the ladder, carrying a sack in which the old man had placed the polyscan. The trek back was substantially easier with the old man shining a light to guide the way.

As he approached the metal rung of steps, Tyler draped the strap of the sack over his head and around his shoulder, letting it rest against his back as he mounted the ladder. He then looked back in the direction of the light, smiled and gave a nod and a wave.

"Get going!" the old man shouted in the distance.

Tyler, replied with a quick, nervous nod and started his ascent.

ONCE he reached the top of the ladder, his eyes were assaulted with the painfully bright light of day. The omnipresent light pierced right through his lids and burned the inside of his head with a fleshy orange fire. He slowly opened the curtains to that cranial cave, gradually letting more of the day gently into his field of vision.

The world was a blazing fog of blue and green and gray, but before long the contours of forms and shadows took shape. He was standing atop a massive white metal surface extending out for hundreds of meters and flanked by what looked to be trees. A clear blue sky was above, in the middle of which were the burning beams of a sun too bright to behold.

A not-so-distant roar of some rushing sound clamored about him. He initially suspected some kind of engine or reactor—perhaps the ship's thrusters. But judging by the trees and his own interior sensations, the ship was at rest—aside from the occasional rumble in his feet. The rushing roar seemed outside the ship itself, but it was hard to tell.

Tyler rubbed his eyes, turned about, and surveyed his surroundings. Beyond the white floor of the ship there was a great winding river extending in two directions, snaking between two great forests of trees. Beyond that, he could make out rolling hills, growing eventually into great mountains. In every direction he looked, he saw nothing but an untouched landscape of vegetation, and occasional distant bodies of water.

Looking back down to the floor upon which he now stood, the glowing ivory surface of the ship clashed with that scenic vista. It was like an inverted shadow, blotting out the beauty of his surroundings and its glorious complexity with the simplicity of vulgar graffiti. It was as though someone in spite had quickly defaced a masterpiece with a bucket of white paint.

Now to attend to the task at hand—if only to see the rest of that natural glory around him.

The old man had told Tyler there should be an emergency egress hatch on the port side of the stern edge of the ship, immediately adjacent to the propulsion thruster assembly, before the fuselage sloped down to the port side foil. Tyler wasn't sure if he completely understood how to find said hatch based on the old man's directions, but he felt reticent to interrupt him at the time.

Tyler walked in one direction towards what seemed like the most obvious "edge" he could find. And as he drew near, he become increasingly aware of how much of an edge it was indeed. A sharp drop directly to the bottom of the ship, where he could see the rushing waves of the river at least a hundred meters below.

He backed away from that precipice with a gulp and then carefully walked parallel to it, keeping a comfortable dis-

tance from the edge. Something then caught his eye. It was strangely red, staining the surface of the ship like drops of blood. When he was suitably close, he could see it was writing.
"EMERGENCY HATCH."

After cranking the large red wheel affixed to the top of the dome, and peeling the heavy lid back, Tyler exposed the hatch. Inside was a long tubular shaft running down the height of the ship. At first, it appeared to be a simple semicircular groove cut into the outside of the ship with metal rungs running down it. Upon closer examination, the flicker of distortion revealed transparent platforms at regular intervals along with a curved outward facing transparent wall.

He stared down that long hatchway with trepidation, coming to sense a fear of heights that was as-of-yet unrealized. A gust of wind caught him by surprise, ever so slightly—yet suddenly—pushing him toward that abyss. The shock set his heart racing as he gripped the hatch door for support.

With a slow blink and a sigh, he made his descent. Right step. Release. Drop. Left step. Between the strain of his aching limbs, the weight on his back from the sack, and the vertigo between his ears, his head was pounding again.

"Just don't look down," he told himself. A comforting mantra he recalled instinctively from he knew not where. It seemed to help, and before long he was halfway done with his slow methodical descent.

Around the midpoint of his climb down, Tyler braved a step out toward one of the glass-like platforms. There he stopped and caught his breath. Standing upon that clear floor, looking out towards the clear wall, he could see more clearly the vista beyond. The winding river, glistening with sunlight. Nearby tree tops coming into view below. The roaring sound had quieted when he entered the shaft, but now it was yet louder. There was little doubt that it came from something below.

When Tyler finally reached the bottom of the shaft, the transparent wall had ended. He stood on a small metal grated walkway that jutted out from the ship's exterior. At this point, the rushing roar was louder than ever, and also unmistakable. Water. The thunderous murmur of some smoldering current. A strangely large sound. Louder and more violent than the peaceful river appeared.

Even directly beneath his feet, the river seemed relatively tranquil. There was a small smattering of rapids here and there near shallow outcroppings of rock in the distance, but nothing substantial. Nevertheless, the crashing clamor was close to deafening.

Tyler took off his sack and knelt down, opening the bag to retrieve the polyscan. As his fingers felt through the contents of the bag, they came across something else he didn't immediately recognize. He carefully withdrew the object, revealing an emergency kit.

"Heh," he noted to himself with amusement, as he thought back to the cranky curmudgeon. The old man had a minimum of concern for him after all, it would seem.

Tyler slid the kit back into the pack, withdrew the polyscan in its place, and set himself to work scanning the ship's exterior as he slowly sauntered along the walkway. As he did, he knew he was only delaying the inevitable. At some point, he was going to have to take some readings from farther away to increase the line of sight.

He eyed the water below, distracted by its undulations as he scanned the ship. He finally stepped back to the ladder, and then passed it a pace or two to the edge of the ship's fuselage. The river bank was less than ten meters from where he stood.

He gazed out at the waves lapping at that rugged tree-lined shore as he put the polyscan back into the sack and rose to his feet purposefully.

It seemed close enough. He would just need to give it a good toss to get across. But once he did, he would be committed. And getting across the water himself would be the necessary next step. With a sigh, he swung the sack back to build momentum.

Just as he was about to release the pack into the air, he stopped himself. With a jerk of his own motions like a train coming to a sudden halt, he twitched and shook, upsetting his own balance in the process. With another sigh and a shake of the head, he reproved his own folly. There was no telling how sensitive the device would be or if it could survive such a trip. What was he thinking?

After a moment's thought, Tyler decided to remove his jumpsuit. He carefully sat down and unstrapped his boots, setting them aside along with his socks. As he began unzipping his suit, he became acutely aware of something hanging around his neck. A kind of chain draped down his chest, and nestled amidst a wisp of hair lay a pendant. Tyler fondled it, turning it over with his fingers, as he slowly inspected it. It was in the shape of a perfect circle, bisected by a line segment. No discernible inscriptions. A simple glittering gold pendant. And no real idea what it could mean.

After stripping off his jumpsuit, he stuffed it in the pack, arranging it around the polyscan and the kit. He then stood up and stared off at the shore, turned to look at his boots, and then turned back to the shore. Thought for a moment. And then he looked down to his shorts. With a sigh and a shrug, he took them off too.

After some careful arrangement, he managed to fit his boots into the sack with the polyscan and the kit, carefully wedging his undershorts and socks in between everything for make-shift padding. He sighed and scratched the back of his head. It seemed like he was forgetting something.

"Oh," Tyler remarked to himself as he returned his attention to the pendant around his neck. He rubbed its slick surface between his thumb and index finger, looking it over again, before removing the necklace and placing it in the bag.

Standing naked from head to toe in the mild breeze of a temperate day, he closed his eyes and felt the cool air lick his bare skin. He breathed out a sigh, gathered up the pack, and slung it with a more than moderate amount of strength to ensure it passed the water. It landed and tumbled through the scrub near the shore before settling in some underbrush.

Now it was his turn…

Dangling from the walkway, less than two meters above the surface of the river, Tyler dipped his toes to test the water. It was somewhat cool, but far from freezing. He let the waves tickle his feet for a moment more, before breathing in a deep gulp of air, closing his eyes, grabbing his nose with one hand and letting go with the other.

His entire body slipped into the river. The moment the top of his head sank beneath the waves, his feet touched down on the soft riverbed below. The sudden immersion shocked his nerves, sending sweeping shivers over his quaking tensed up flesh. He instinctively drew his arms in, one hand still holding his nose. Slightly curled in a partial fetal position, Tyler took a beat or two to adjust before quickly extending out and starting to swim.

The motions came instinctively as he gracefully pushed off from that mud gravel floor and swung his arms around, cupping water with his hands, gliding through his liquid surroundings as smoothly as a fish. A current gently pushed him from one side, but he swam against it to compensate.

In a moment or two, Tyler emerged from the river, climbing from its shallow depths onto the scrub shelf of the river bank. Raising himself erect, he wiped the wetness from his eyes, ran his fingers through his soggy hair and reviewed his environs. Once he recaptured his bearings, he headed toward the bit of shrubbery where he tossed his pack.

He breathed a sigh of relief when he found the sack where he expected it. He shook a little to shake off the dampness from his trembling flesh. Wiped the sinewy folds of flesh with his hands to help. Reached down to the crevasse near his inner thigh and wiped where it seemed wettest. And then combed his hair with his fingers, squeezing and wringing the locks. One more shake and he would be just dry enough to get dressed.

Tyler rifled through the sack and retrieved his shorts, jumpsuit, socks, and boots. He hurriedly dressed to warm his now shivering skin. By the time he slipped on his second boot, the ground started to rumble...

Alarmed, Tyler jumped to his feet and frantically looked about. A low metal groan bellowed from the ship. When he turned to face it, there was a loud crackling pop followed by a plume of smoke toward the top of the giant vessel. A series of groans followed, and the ground then started to shake more and more with violence.

Tyler instinctively started to run along the river bank away from the ship. When he had put some distance between it and himself he turned back, gasping for breath, to behold—in horror!—the entire ship quickly slipping out of sight below the horizon...

Slowly he hiked back to his position and then further on a few dozen meters or so to finally come to the edge of the world. The river flooded out into a waterfall. And as he peered down into the abyss of that giant cataract, his view was clouded by a massive mist spewing up from some unseen bottom.

The ship was gone.

IT was close to half an hour before he could even begin to process the loss. Pacing down the river. Peering over the edge. Then pacing back again. Pacing the other way. Sitting occasionally and watching the water rush by. Staring at his own forlorn face in the water. A handsome face of bittersweet beauty, draped as it was in fear and sadness. He ran his hands through his hair in quiet desperation and listened to the loudest silence he'd ever heard in the roar of the rushing waves.

There, in the midst of despair and grief, he wept bitter tears. Partly for himself and his situation, but mostly for the man he met. He hardly knew the man, but in some way that only made it worse. Could he have done something different? Something more?

He finally found himself sitting at the water's edge, inviting in silence. Letting the clamor drown out his thoughts. Somehow he knew he had to. He let it wash away his worry and fear—and to some extent even his grief for the time. Peace came to him in the form of a single thought: *When all is lost and nothing's left, anywhere else is right.*

It came like a half-remembered quote from the hazy dream of his forgotten past. A past that—like the ship to which it was tenuously tethered—was washed away into a misty chasm. Washed away. Cleansed. It left the landscape pure and uncomplicated. Even when it came with a cost, there was yet freedom in the future.

He rose to his feet, with his eyes closed. Breathed out a deep cleansing sigh. Opened his eyes, looked about the trees and shrubs, with his back now to the river. He chose a direction on a whim, and set out on a hike. Strapping his pack on tight—the bag of all his meager possessions—and walked forward into the forest. *I have been a stranger in a strange land.*

That one he was almost certain was a quote. Its source again unknown. Yet stranger than the novelty of this new landscape was its strange familiarity. Green trees with brown bark. A blue sky with a blazing sun and a passing cloud or two. Names came into his head for these things. Even for the winged creatures he saw occasionally gliding above and between the canopy overhead. Birds. At least that's what came to mind when he saw their distant silhouettes. Would that same word come to mind if he saw one closer?

It was as though he were walking on the edge of something in his soul, not unlike the crest of the cataract somewhere in the distance to his right. This strange straddling sensation of feeling familiar and yet exploring something completely new. Fear and mourning on one side. Calm and confidence on the other. It all bubbled up a new word to his consciousness: *Adventure.*

The pounding in his head returned. Tyler walked toward a small clearing, sat down in the middle of it, and reviewed the contents of his bag. Polyscan and emergency kit. The former was next to useless now. For all of its technological complexity, it was little more than dead weight at this point. A relic of some other time. A relic of some civilization that, for him, was no more. Still, there was a place for relics. The mundane and the sublime. Impractical aspirations still had a practical purpose: Hope.

Nodding solemnly to himself, Tyler gently set the polyscan aside and pulled out the kit. With a click, it popped open, revealing its contents. Multispray. Torchgun. Spool of gauze. Hydrofilter. Bandages. The names all came to him as he reviewed the assorted items. The words popped into his consciousness like inspiration, giving him a little surprise with each revelation.

He picked out the gauze and wrapped some around his head and tied it off. Once he was done, he carefully placed each item into its designated place reverently like an ancient priest replacing a series of fetishes back into a sacred chest. The kit was his ark, and it would carry him through this sea of trees. Or at least, he hoped. And so at last he placed hope itself into the pack, returning the polyscan along with the kit, side by side in his sack.

The sound of the river and its crashing cataract carried through the forest for some time. It seemed like hours before it finally faded. He thought of changing directions. But it would be so easy to get lost in this sea of flora. He would look to the sun for guidance. And over time that bright star was slowly sinking in the sky, leading him towards its descent.

When the sun was nearly set, twinkling between the tree trunks, the land gently sloped down and the trees then quickly parted. Sparkling in the distance was something familiar. Water. A wide open lake. Gentle waves in a cool breeze.

He jogged the rest of the way. He couldn't say why exactly, if he even bothered to ask himself. Something about that distant shoreline strangely lifted his spirit. Perhaps it was simply his growing sense of thirst, but it seemed like something more. Some whisper of hope was there.

Tyler sat down to catch his breath on the quiet shoreline of that tranquil lake. And once he did, breathed in its beauty. Distant flapping shapes floated by in the sky. A soft silent draft of wind swept along the water, delicately licking the lake's skin. The sun shone beyond a curtain of trees on the distant shore. Everything was tinged with the golden glow of twilight.

He remembered his thirst and so attended to the bag. Rifling back through his belongings, something tickled his fingertips. He reached down in a moment of curiosity and pulled out a chain. The amulet. He had almost forgotten…

All the more gold in the golden light, the pendant glittered in his hand as he fondled it with his thumb. With a sigh and a shake of his head, he returned it to the pack and pulled out the emergency kit. Retrieving the hydrofilter, Tyler set about the work of suctioning out a liter of water from the lake before swiftly glugging down nearly half of that into himself.

His thirst momentarily abated, Tyler returned his attention to the scene before him. The sun was setting quickly and the light of day was failing. And with the darkness would come cold. Some day *his* light would fail. Some day, his warmth would be gone. Would he just disappear into mist like the old man? Mist came to his eyes with the thought, and he rubbed it away with a sad sniff.

He didn't know if anything in the world was even edible. At least not *this* world. He had the vague recollection of eating before. He must have. Digestion and growth over a course of years of maturation. Yet another body of facts that floated in the hazy recollection at the back of his mind, disconnected from any specific moments of time, space and sensation.

How long could a man go without eating? For some reason, the word "desert" came to his mind when he asked himself that question. Yet this was no desert he was in. At least not by any outward appearance. And somehow his surroundings kept him from entertaining too seriously the looming threat of death. Graceful greens. Glorious golds. Beauty radiated in all directions and poured over into his soul, warmly washing him with peace.

When the sky finally darkened and the stars started to show themselves, the wind turned cold and Tyler knew he had to act. He cleared out an area and dug a shallow pit. He then gathered together kindling of assorted sticks and grasses, and found a log or two of deadwood drifting in the lake. With the torchgun from his pack, he lit a fire in the small makeshift pit. He even managed to find a handful of larger rocks here and there, which he bundled together around the pit to help seal in the radiating heat.

By the time he was done, the advent of night was complete. The wind had stopped, but the cold remained. The lake was now a serene mirror of the heavens above. The trees were black silhouettes carved out of a sea of stars. Blazing pinpricks of light like distant fires in the great beyond. The embers of his own campfire rose up in sparks, rising and dying in the starlight of those distant heavens.

Now he only wished he had someone with whom to share this warmth. As his flesh tingled with the surrounding heat, his heart ached with bitter cold. Would he ever see another human soul again?

THE world slowly materialized as a blur of light, as Tyler awoke from a dreamless sleep. It felt like something had knocked against his side. The dull pain of a quick but soft kick emanated from his ribs. Then it came again. Another knock, against his bicep this time. And then he heard it. A smooth soft voice—but a demanding one.

"I said get up!"

Tyler sat up in a flash, then subsequently rose to his feet before his eyes fully adjusted. It was a steely-eyed woman with a Volcund-class plasma pistol. He instinctively stepped back and started to raise his hands.

"That's right, keep those hands up!" she barked.

His heart was pounding in his ears now, and he knew he had to slow it down. He took long even breaths, instinctively seeking calm in the storm of his own panic. The threat sent him into a state of hyper-awareness. He darted his eyes here and there, quickly assessing the situation.

She couldn't be any more than 170 centimeters, probably less. Her right hand was holding the pistol, supported by the palm of her left. But her elbows were tucked in, not fully extended as they should be. The angle was too low. She wasn't really aiming the gun. It was more like a shield, her arms tucked in defensively.

He glanced down to her feet. They were slightly spread apart, but not very staggered at all. In fact, her left foot was very slightly in front of her right. A subtle tremor was there.

Her face was all intimidation. Cold hazel eyes beneath a furrowed brow. But even there, there were signs. Her chin was bent down. Her lips tucked in. When he managed to quiet his breath, he could hear hers.

"I don't want any trouble," he said in an even voice as he slowly stepped back.

"That's far enough!"

Tyler replied with a nod and a slow blink.

"Who are you? What are you doing out here?"

"My name is… Tyler. As far as what I'm doing…" he slowly exhaled. Where to begin? Not that there was much to tell. His short life flashed before his eyes. Such a strange short life. Filled with so much confusion and uncertainty. He might as well have been born yesterday. And if he was to die today, what had any of it meant? To lose the ship and gain his life, only to lose it again. What was his life before? Had he had a life before? Or was that some residue left over from something else—someone else—that he just inherited? Perhaps the world was a dream. Was he the dreamer?

In many ways, he had already died. He lost so much of he knew not what. And then he lost again that which he knew. Perhaps his mourning the loss of the ship and his only acquaintance would seem completely absurd if he could remember anything from the life before. Perhaps that ship was just a prison he had escaped. Perhaps that old man he now found himself missing was his jailer.

Before he could start to explain, the woman was starting to crouch down. She kept her eyes focused on him, pistol extended in her right hand, as she bent with her knees toward his pack. She reached in and started to pull something out. He heard the rattling of a chain.

She glanced down, and suddenly her eyes widened. His heart raced into action, as he noted that her eyes were completely transfixed now on the amulet. She started to gasp at the sight. And at that, he knew he had to act immediately.

Tyler rushed in and tackled her to the ground, gripping her right wrist with his right hand as he turned himself around and pinned her down with his back. He knew this way he could keep his vitals directed away from the now screaming woman.

"No, no no, no no, noo!!" she called out and screeched as he slammed her hand down, forcing her to release the pistol. He then scrambled to his feet as she clawed at him. Just as he managed to kick the pistol several meters away, he felt a sudden sharp pain on his back.

"Gahh!" he growled in pain as her teeth sank into his shoulder's flesh.

He dropped to his knees, and they began to wrestle wildly. He managed to get her into a nelson hold, lying on his back, one arm between her arm and the back of her neck, with the other coming between her neck and breast.

"Are we—are we… done?" he asked, struggling to catch his breath. His question was met with panting. Otherwise, she remained silent. *Like a lamb to the slaughter*, he thought. And the thought moved him to great pity.

"Ma'am, I'm—I'm sorry. I—I did what I had to do," he said, still struggling to catch his breath while the woman sank into his heaving chest. She was still silent.

"I really meant it when I said I don't want any trouble," he continued. Silence.

He sighed, still holding her locked in place, arms gripped tightly with his legs wrapped around her hips. Once his breathing started to slow, he heard it. Some kind of muttering whispers. The sound seemed oddly familiar.

He needed to get her off of him. He needed neutrality. How he would do that was going to require finesse and speed. So he planned it out, took a breath and rolled her to one side, as he rolled himself and hopped to his feet as quickly as possible—half expecting a tussle or some mad scramble towards the distant pistol.

But... nothing. She stayed curled up in a ball where he left her, shaking softly, continuing to mutter. But her posture was deliberate now. Her face to the ground, cupped in her hands. Her knees tucked beneath her trembling torso.

And so he decided to sit. He let himself slowly collapse to the ground. One leg tucked beneath the other while resting himself on his hands, he caught his breath for a moment. And then he stayed in the silence, carefully keeping his eyes on the woman, looking for any signs of stirring. But she continued in that posture, continuing to whisper. To herself? To...? A word for it seemed to float at the edge of his consciousness, but it wouldn't drift in.

But another word did glide into his mind. Beauty. He hadn't taken note of it before, but she was truly beautiful. Delicate curves gently sloping down toward a soft curtain of deep rich amber hair. Her pitiable posture made him long to see her face again. In part to see her fears allayed, and in part just to behold her countenance once more.

The murmur stopped. She was truly silent now. And then she rose to her feet and slowly turned to face him. He swallowed at the sight and thought quickly about his next actions. He had an instinct to stand with her. It would perhaps be the more cautious thing to do. She still could be dangerous, to be sure. It might also convey some measure of respect.

He decided to stay seated. He was slightly closer to the weapon. It *probably* wouldn't make a huge difference in the event of a mad scramble. And in the mean time, allowing her to tower over him might help convey his amiable intentions.

"I… really just want peace," he finally uttered.

"You all say that. I've seen the kind of *peace* you people bring," she replied with more than a hint of derision amidst her trembling voice. She had piercing eyes of flame. He shuddered at the sight of those fiery jade eyes. His soul was filled at once with fear and admiration. She was a green-eyed goddess turning on him in judgment. And he was in awe.

"Wha-what… *people*, exactly?" Tyler asked hesitantly.

"The Dominion, of course. Don't play the fool with me."

"I, uh… the Dominion?"

"I saw your necklace. That Kyrian trinket. The only Kyrians in this sector are with the Dominion."

He averted his eyes and darted them around, struggling to recall. The words sounded strangely familiar, but they danced outside the spotlight of consciousness, mocking him in the dark. Kyrian? Dominion? Before he could begin to respond, she continued.

"*Peace.* You speak of love and peace. But it comes at the edge of a sword. It always has. And especially so with you Dominionists." Her voice was trembling with some mixture of fear and anger.

"I… really wish I knew what you were talking about," he uttered as a lament.

She responded with a scoff and a piercing stare. A tense silence sat between them. And despair creeped up on him as though from behind. Tyler was trapped in that moment with no idea how to proceed. His eyes started to well up. A touch of self-pity mixed with a good amount of frustration. How could he convince this woman? The only person left in his life, and here he was trapped in her animosity.

Something strange happened then. Out of the corner of his eye, he saw her gaze off into the distance at the weapon lying on the ground and then turn back to him before slowly lowering herself onto a nearby stone—one of the stones he had erected the night prior.

He looked up to see her studying him with narrowed eyes, cocking her head this way and that, her lovely locks fluttering ever so slightly as she did. He averted his eyes again. Closed them. Waited in desperate anticipation.

"Okay… so just who do you say that you are, then?" she asked with a fair amount of skepticism, with only the slightest tinge of genuine curiosity.

He looked up and let out a sigh. "To be completely honest, I… don't… know…"

"Hah!" she laughed mockingly. "You told me a name earlier! What was it? Tyson? Dylan?"

"Tyler."

"Tyler. Right. So you admit it."

"It's a name I learned yesterday. From… an old man," Tyler replied, gazing off into the forest mournfully.

"Amnesia? Is that what you're claiming? You people spout some seriously stupid bullshit, but this takes the cake. Is that what this ridiculous getup is about with the head wrap?" Her scornful remark was followed with an outburst of laughter.

There was nothing he could say in reply to her mocking. And so he stayed silent. *Like a lamb to the slaughter.* And like before, the thought moved him to pity. For himself this time.

After a moment or two of quiet, Tyler slowly raised his eyes to see her gently stroking her cheek with her index finger as she gazed off to the side in quiet contemplation. Crystal eyes between two occasionally squinting lids perched above a gently sloping nose. Soft salmon lips, slightly pursed. Finally, she parted those lips and spoke.

"Alright, so maybe there's a way we can get to the truth. You had a polyscan in that sack, right?"

"Right. Yes. Why?"

"Do you want to hand it over, Amensia Boy?"

"Uh, o-okay." He reached for the nearby sack and opened it.

"Slowly," she demanded.

After he carefully retrieved the polyscan, he tossed it her way. With an eye roll and a sigh, she turned it on and started to tap through assorted interfaces on the screen.

"Here you are," she said as turned the screen toward him.

TYLER, JONAH C.
Special Consultant
Personnel ID 3-307-582

There he saw next to his name a face he recognized. His own. But it was different from the one he remembered staring back at him in the water. It was somehow more serious. Stern, and knowing. Nevertheless, the features were there.

"Jonah?" he whispered in awe.

His question was met with another eye roll. But he hadn't seen it. His own eyes were transfixed in the distance. Jonah? Yesterday in his trek to the lake he had wondered about his name. He had actually entertained the notion that perhaps "Tyler" was a surname. But then, why had the old man called him "Johnny?"

"Now, Mister Jonah, how about we look at this wound of yours, eh?"

"Okay..." he replied with a bit of confusion. He had no idea the polyscan was so versatile. She tapped away at the screen for a moment, before raising it purposely towards his face.

"Heh, as I suspected. Completely superficial. Effectively a scratch."

To this remark, Tyler furrowed his brow and parted his lips as though he was about to say something. Although he had no words for a reply. If the wound had nothing to do with it, then… what? But the moment didn't last long, before she continued.

"Wait… what's this?" the woman asked herself with a strange mix of concern and curiosity.

"What? What is it?"

"There's… something, hmm…" and then she gasped slightly, before continuing. "Heh… wow."

"What did you find?" he asked impatiently.

"This," the woman replied as she turned the screen to Tyler.

He couldn't quite make out what he was seeing. It looked like a medical image of… his head? Before he could ask for clarification, she volunteered an explanation.

"It's an implant. A pretty extensive one, too. The hypocrisy never ends."

"I…" Tyler started before letting out a sigh of frustration. "I don't understand."

She stared off to the side and flitted her eyes around in thought for a moment, and then stated with a slow rocking nod, "And you may very well be telling the truth at that."

"What do you mean?"

"I've heard rumors about this kind of thing. Dominion Intelligence. Voluntary lobotomies."

"Are you implying I've been… lobotomized?" He frowned at the suggestion. Perhaps he misrecalled the meaning, but he was pretty sure he hadn't suffered a literal lobotomy.

"Hyperbole, to be sure. Well…" she peered into his eyes for a moment. "At least in your case. But… some kind of controlled memory loss? It's entirely possible. And… it would explain why you let me scan you."

He breathed a sigh of relief.

"But then it could still be an elaborate rouse."

He breathed a sigh of frustration.

They sat in silence for a moment or two, before the silence was broken. A low churning growl from Tyler's abdomen. "You wouldn't happen to have anything to eat, would you…?" he asked meekly.

She stared at him in silence for a moment, shifting her head slowly back and forth, as she stared at him from the corners of her eyes. She let her gaze fall and then sighed. "This way."

Without another word, she handed the polyscan to him and headed to the water's edge. There she retrieved her pistol. She gazed at him one more time, and he replied with a nervous gulp. She then holstered the gun, turned and gestured for him to follow. He hurriedly gathered up his belongings and jogged after her.

They briskly hiked along the water's edge for several minutes as the lake started to slowly bend. He didn't ask where she was leading him. It was his turn to show a little faith. And for that opportunity he was grateful enough.

At the end of their short sojourn, slowly emerging from a thicket in the distance was some complication of metal and glass. It was a ship. A sleek modest-sized vessel with a clear cabin fit for one or two. Descending from that cabin was a rung of steps.

"Wait here," she commanded, as she climbed the short ladder into the craft.

Tyler obeyed, waiting nearby as the woman retrieved a pair of pouches. As she descended the steps, she tossed one to him.

He wasted no time in tearing it open and devouring its contents. It was a mixture of some kind. Raisins? Nuts? Something like that. He didn't bother to identify what he was eating. The moment the first bite hit his tongue, he became keenly aware of how ravenously hungry he really was.

"Heh…" she muttered with a smirk and a cocked eyebrow.

"M-thank you!" he exclaimed between voracious munches and crunches.

She replied with a nod and a guarded smile.

When he was done, and just starting to lick his fingers, she asked, "What do you remember about that ship of yours? What does it look like?"

"Oh, well, it uh… wait… I never mentioned a ship," he replied, narrowing his eyes. At that moment, he was a little proud of himself for his shrewdness. But that pride quickly faded away when she chuckled and shook her head in return.

"If this *is* a rouse, it's a really thorough one. You'd have to be pretty good at playing dumb."

He replied with a confused scowl and sigh.

She continued, "There's only one settlement on this planet, and you're not part of it. I know you came here on a vessel, and I'm pretty sure I know which one."

"And if you're wrong?" he asked.

"I doubt I will be—unless you lie," she replied.

And he could lie at that. But then, she might see through it, and that could make matters worse. And if he did divulge the truth, he wasn't entirely sure what its significance might be. After a brief moment, he decided to trust his fate to the truth. In the end, it was better than trusting it to a lie.

"I know it was a lot larger than yours," he said, gesturing to her craft. "At least 15, 20, floors, I think. Blazingly white. Sloping face. Wings. I have a hazy memory of a wedge kind of shape. But honestly I never got a chance to see the whole thing all at once, before… well, before it was gone."

"Gone?"

"Yeah…"

Over the span of a few minutes, he told her the story of his life. He had had a short life thus far, so it made a short story, but he told her most of the details he could recall nevertheless. The ascent in the dark. Meeting the old man. His journey up and down to scan the ship. His immersion in the river. His watching the ship fall below the horizon. And finally his trek to the lake.

"And that's when I met *you*," he said with a nervous chuckle.

He had a child like innocence about him. An eccentric, but warm, enthusiasm. A boyish charm. She wasn't sure how to feel about it. She wasn't sure how to feel about *him*. She decided to trust her intuition. And so once he was done with his rambling tale, she broke the lingering silence.

"My name is Anne."

"Pleasure to meet you, Miss Anne," he said with a reserved grin.

"I suppose I should tell you why I neglected to introduce myself before."

He nodded and leaned against the fuselage of her craft, matching her own posture.

"I know the ship you described. I met up with it in the air before… it… shot me down."

He quietly gasped and furrowed his brow. She gave a subtle knowing smile, before looking back off to the side and continuing.

"I had left the station on a routine survey. I noted an upper atmospheric disturbance on the scanner and called it in. I pursued investigating the disturbance which turned out to be your ship making a fast-burn entry. Considering how unusual that was, I checked the EM transceiver and discovered a distress signal on the emergency band along with an ongoing transmission—audio only. I couldn't make out what was being said. Seemed like some kind of… cacophony… of voices.

"So I, uh, approached the ship once it had slowed enough from the friction. I attempted contact over the com, but… nothing. Just the sounds of some kind of chaos as far as I could tell. The ship looked just like you described. Merchant class. Star freighter. No particular insignias.

"Once I got close enough, that's when it happened. Single blast to the starboard engine compartment. Put the craft out of commission pretty quick. I practically had to *glide* down to the lake here.

"I spent the afternoon getting a lay of the land. Com was knocked out, so all I have—heh, all *we* have I guess—is a beacon. We don't have much of a satellite network here yet on Solus 4, so the beacon has to work by topographical analysis to get positioning."

"Solus 4…" he whispered to himself.

"So… I guess I'm ready when you are."

"Ready? For… what?"

"To set up the beacon. There's a hill about twenty minutes from here." She pointed at a gentle mound rising from the trees in what looked like only a short distance away. "It should give us enough height to get an extrusion map."

"What happens then?"

"Then we wait for help to arrive."

"Help?"

"I'm assuming you don't want to be stuck out here in the wilderness any more than I do. It shouldn't take long before someone back at the station picks up the signal and comes out to our position."

"Right, right… okay…"

THE slow march up the distant sloping hill was a fairly uneventful one. Anne had gathered together a pack of her own containing some assorted supplies—along with the beacon—and headed out quite promptly. Tyler followed with some unspoken trepidation. What would this "station" be like? Who would pick them up and how? Would encountering these new people be as *dramatic* as his meeting with Anne?

Over the course of the quiet walk, he forgot about his fear for a time as he took in the slowly shifting surroundings. Meandering between tranquil trees. Watching the light of the sun trickle through a dancing mosaic of leaves above. Listening to the chirping songs of distant birds. Breathing in the aroma of—pine?—wafting through the great columns of tree trunks. Columns that rose up from the forest floor like the supports of some vast ancient temple. The blue heaven above was its domed roof. The fresh smell drifting on the wind was like incense.

Silence walked between them. It was as though they both could sense the sacred ground upon which they trod. Were all forests like this? Tyler could recall the word, but not the experience. Yet from all he knew, sacred sites were usually buildings for some reason. But what art or artifice could compare with the sanctity of his surroundings? He felt it since the moment he climbed from the bowels of that ship. He felt it again when he emerged from the water of the river. To navigate this landscape was its own pilgrimage, where the journey was its own destination.

When they finally reached the top of the hill, they came to a clearing. Anne set up the beacon. A tripod of sorts with a diamond-shaped device at its top, standing about a meter and a half tall. When she turned it on, the diamond-shaped contraption lit up, but otherwise nothing else obvious happened.

"And now we wait," Anne remarked.

Tyler replied with a nod, and took his first real look around. From this vantage point, the horizon stretched out for several dozen kilometers at least. In the distance, he could see the lake, and further on he spotted the massive waterfall where his life began. It was at the edge of a grand curving basin.

"There…" Tyler stated, in quiet awe, as he pointed out the giant cataract in the distance.

"Wellington Falls."

"Wellington?"

"Dr. Wellington was one of the engineers reviewing the data back from the first probes to Solus 4. I think she was the first one to point it out."

"Oh."

"I was actually on my way to survey it before the crash. Pretty remarkable, isn't it?"

"Yeah…" he whispered.

He sat in silence, listening to the breeze. She shared some water from her canteen and another snack. She fidgeted with some equipment. A quarter-hour passed before a speck appeared on the distant horizon, away from where they had been.

"Listen…" she said with a sigh. "I can't risk the security of the station. I'm going to need you to wear this…" She was holding several cable ties and a bundle of cloth in her hands.

"What is that? What do you mean?"

"Restraints. Or the best I can make of them. And this spare cloth can double as a blindfold, I think."

He nodded soberly. "I think I understand."

With that, Anne gestured for Tyler to stand up and turn around. He complied. Delicate fingers grasped his wrist and gently pulled his hand behind his back. She fastened one tie around his wrist, then another, and then strapped them both together with a third. It wasn't terribly uncomfortable that way, despite the harsh edges of the polymer bands.

She then came a little closer, her soft belly almost touching his tied up hands as she reached up to his head. He felt a soothing warmth radiating from her body as she stood behind him and carefully wrapped the cloth around his eyes and tied it together behind his head.

"There. I… uh… hope that's not too tight."

"I'm okay… thanks."

It wasn't long before he heard a distant hum. A hum that grew louder. After a few minutes, it was a roar. A rushing wind whirled around him violently as the roar rumbled right above him and then beside him. It finally grew suddenly quieter. The rushing spinning whir sound died, letting out a final long whine. A door opened and shut. Footsteps in the near distance.

"What the hell is this?" a man called out with a chuckle.

"Did you get my message?" Anne replied.

"We did, yeah. Gave us a scare for the night. You didn't mention anything about this guy, though."

"I only found him this morning. It's the sovedamned dominion!"

The way she said those words sent a shock of panic straight to Tyler's heart. Had this all been a ruse? Was he going to be summarily executed now that she had an ally? What was the logical next step? He let her tie him up. *Shit.*

"What do you expect to do with him? You got this poor guy tied up like a sovedamned prisoner of war! Are you *trying* to piss off our neighbors?"

"Look, he's a security risk. I have reason to believe he's with Intelligence. And he submitted to the restraints. I actually figured we'd take him back with us. He could use our assistance."

"Is this a freakin' shirt?"

"I used what I had."

The man busted up with laughter. "It's a sovedamned t-shirt!"

Shirt? So that explained the pleasant smell. The faintest whiff of perfume as part of the cloth dangled over Tyler's nose.

"You got a name, buddy?"

"M-me? Yeah, uh… Tyler. J-*Jonah* Tyler, that is."

"C'mon Anne, get that shirt off his face."

"It's a security concern! What if he manages to tell the Dominion where the station is located? Or what if they manage to extract it from his brain, or tort—"

"If they really wanted to find the station, they will. A granular enough image scan over the planet's surface is going to reveal it."

"I don't think we should make it any easier for them."

"The best thing we can do is wait on the Confederation. That and not pissing off—"

"It's okay," Tyler interjected. "If it makes it easier, I'm fine with it… really."

Everyone was hushed for a moment. From the faint sounds of rustling in the still air and the hints of movement he could make out through his makeshift mask, it seemed there was some quick exchange of gestures.

"Alright," the man said, "let's saddle up, I guess."

Through the thin veil of the bottom of the mask/shirt, Tyler could barely make out a bright green sea of trees rushing by below a blinding blue sky. It was a matter of minutes before the craft rapidly slowed and then seemed to hover for a moment before descending straight down.

Once the craft landed, he was led outside. The same delicate fingers which put on his mask now gently removed it. With the dark cloth removed, the bright fiery light of day assaulted his eyes briefly before they momentarily adjusted.

They were in a clearing. A short way off was a row of trees. And between and within those trees, structures. A complex of soft ivory architecture lifted above the forest floor, wrapping around columns of trees with elevated walkways between. The words *elven* and *fairy* came to mind for some reason.

He slowly stepped forward in awe. The structures seemed like some natural outgrowth of the forest, although he knew it could not be so. The off-white color of cream or honeycomb wax. A tranquil hive of humans living in a land of milk and honey. A land of their own making, but still an extension of it.

"Wow…" he gasped.

Anne secretly smiled at his awed expression. The wild-eyed wondrous gaze of a boy. The slack-jawed expression of enthusiasm in one who had never experienced—or one who had forgotten—cynicism. It was infectious. When she turned back to the station, she could almost see it with his eyes.

"This way," she urged as she lightly pressed the back of his forearm.

Tyler was led to the beautiful, strange structures and onto a platform by Anne and the man. The man seemed a bit of a jovial mystery. A bearded figure with some kind of shaded visor over his eyes chewing on what looked like a tooth pick. Now that Tyler got to look at his face, he seemed like a fairly somber type, but his voice betrayed otherwise. Something about the way his bushy mustache obscured the corners of his mouth gave him a constant sullen expression, yet he spoke with a hearty playful warmth.

"So where you taking this poor sap, Anne?"

"I think it's best if we have Ed take a look at him."

"Ed? What about Jenkins?"

"We'll head there next for sure. I have a suspicion I want to confirm first."

"Alright, fair enough. Something to do with the Dominion I take it."

"It's not just the ship, Frank. There's more to it."

"Alright, alright. Taking your word for it."

"Anyways, I'll tell you more about it later."

"Sounds like quite the story. I have a story of my own for you some time."

"Oh?"

"Yeah, last night when you were out goofing off on your camping trip."

She replied with a glare.

Frank chuckled in return.

"Well… it'll have to wait."

Frank nodded and then turned to Tyler, "Jonah, right?"

"Huh? Uh, yeah. Jonah Tyler." He said his name like he was reciting it to himself. Reminding himself, so as not to forget.

"Nice to meet you, Jonah Tyler. Is that just Mister Tyler? Or are you another one of us nerds with too much schooling?"

"Uh… just, uh, you can just call me Tyler… I guess?"

Frank smiled under his bushy beard. "Alright, Tyler. Pleasure meeting you. Frank Hermann. You can just call me Frank."

"Nice to meet you, uh… Frank," Tyler said as he let Frank reach behind his back and awkwardly shake his tied up hand.

After they went their separate ways, Anne escorted Tyler across a network of walkways to the door of one of the beautiful treehouse buildings. After pressing a button immediately adjacent to the door, Anne and Tyler waited a moment before the door slid open.

"Anne! Welcome back! Are you doing okay?"

"Hi, Ed! I'm doing alright, yeah. Frank picked me up shortly after I got the signal out."

"Rode with Frank, eh? I'm surprised you're alive."

They both laughed, before Anne replied, "Well, the ride was a little bumpy, but fortunately I wasn't that far out. Turns out I ended up just a few kilometers out from Wellington Falls, actually."

"Ah, so it *was* a secret vacation after all."

"Heh, I wish. It was a long night… Anyhow, while I was out, I came across Mister Tyler here." With that, Anne stepped aside and gestured to Tyler, who had been standing off out of view.

"Oh, hello there," Ed said in surprise. He then quickly noticed the cable ties strapped behind Tyler's back. "Anne?"

"He's with the Dominion," Anne said with a sigh.

"How can you be sure?"

"He was on that armed merchant ship that fired at me. And I found this…" She pulled out the necklace from Tyler's pack she had been carrying with her.

"I see…"

"Excuse me…" Tyler interjected.

"Hm?" Ed replied.

"What is this place exactly?"

Ed and Anne exchanged glances.

"You… don't know?" Ed asked.

"I'm afraid I don't seem to know much at all," Tyler replied with a sigh.

"He caught me off guard when we met. He… heh… well to be honest, Mister Tyler, you scared the life out of me. I thought I was going to die."

Tyler hung his head in shame.

Anne continued, "But… I'm sure I gave him quite the scare myself. I had my plasma pistol trained on him." She scratched the back of her neck and sighed.

"Wow… sounds, uh, intense," Ed replied and furrowed his brow.

"Well, anyhow, the point is I think we have a bit of… tentative trust. He claims to have lost his memory. And I did find something peculiar when I scanned him. A cerebral implant…"

"Ah, I see why you came to me then."

"Indeed. I wanted to be sure, and thought maybe you could do some more extensive analysis."

"Alright, well, come on in. And let's get these makeshift shackles off you, eh?"

After a moment, they were ushered in, and the door was closed and locked. Tyler's restraints were promptly cut and tossed aside. He massaged his wrists a bit as he examined his surroundings. A well-lit interior with an assortment of screens, several chairs, and some kind of peculiar cushioned table like a reclining bed, but with some manner of contraption encircling the top.

"So, I don't think we've been properly introduced. Mister Tyler, was it?"

"Uh, yes. Jonah Tyler," Tyler replied, again reciting the words to remind himself.

"Oh, uh, Mister Tyler, this is Doctor Edward Reed. He is our resident cyberneticist," Anne said, gesturing to Ed.

"Heh, thank you for that, Doctor Anima Chinguun," Ed said with a smirk. Then turning back to Tyler, "You can just call me Ed."

Tyler thought for a moment, then blurted out to Anne, "C-can you call me… Jonah?"

Anne and Ed exchanged raised eyebrows. The way he had asked it was as if he were a child asking for permission. Anne replied "Uh, sure… Jonah."

Jonah softly smiled and nodded. He liked the sound of that name. *Jonah.* For some reason, hearing that name on *her* lips in particular sent little waves of peace through his body.

"So, Mister Jonah, if you'd like to follow me, perhaps we could take a look at that head of yours, eh?"

Jonah nodded as Ed led him to the reclining cushioned table in the room. He slid his head into the scanning apparatus as instructed, and Ed began tapping away on something while Jonah did his best to relax.

Several minutes passed while Ed quietly worked the nearby console. He would occasionally let out a "Hmm…" or an "Interesting…" while working. Jonah was starting to get a little claustrophobic with his head stuck in that shelled out tube of a device. Ed finally slid the tube off Jonah's head and gestured for him to rise and follow Ed to his workstation.

"See this?" Ed asked, shifting his eyes between Jonah and Anne while pointing out a complex blob of something on his screen.

"Yeah?"

"Right behind this anterior lobe attachment on the hippocampus. That's a Mark 5 inhibitor."

"And in Kinmish?" Anne asked as she gestured folding her arms.

"Y'know… I'm gonna have to remember that one the next time you start prattling on about cell cultures or whatever weird shit you biochemists are into."

Anne chuckled. "I just have to give you tech guys grief."

"Okay, so the name is actually fairly self-explanatory. The inhibitor is a complex network of nanotech centered around the hippocampus that's capable of very selectively targeting mnemonic patterns. It *inhibits* recall."

"Wow… so this really exists."

"Oh yeah, definitely. It's bleeding edge technology. I've only ever seen a Mark 2 before in person, and the 5 is something of a rumor. You can find early prototypes and older models on the black market in very rare circumstances, but by and large this is definitely something only used in Intelligence. I had to have special elevated clearance just to see that Mark 2 behind an enclosure. That was back when I had a short stint as an Intelligence Contractor with the Confederation."

"So what's being inhibited precisely?"

"Well, based on what I can tell of how this implant is configured to function, I would surmise that nearly all episodic memory and a good chunk of semantic memory. It looks like it's specifically tuned to any declarative memory that relates to personal identity. It's obviously not doing much to affect procedural memory."

"Obviously how?"

"Well, if his procedural memory were greatly impacted he wouldn't really be able to walk, talk, eat, et cetera."

"Ah…"

"Can you take it out?" Jonah interjected.

"Oh boy…" Ed said with an exasperated sigh, "I… honestly wouldn't know where to begin with that. For one thing, this is continuously operating. A spider web of nanites effectively tangled up in your synapses. Direct physical extraction wouldn't be feasible without some very likely, uh…" Ed trailed off as his eyes darted around the screen for a couple of moments.

"Some likely what?" Jonah asked impatiently.

"Oh, well… some serious brain damage in all likelihood." After a moment of mournful silence, Ed continued, "But on the flip side, these devices have a reset option in place that restores the mnemonic pathways for recall. You're supposed to be able to basically flip a switch and everything comes back."

"So you just have to… flip a switch?" Jonah asked earnestly.

"Well… that's a figure of speech of course. And there's a huge caveat here."

"Encryption," Anne interjected.

"Right. Yes. These things were designed to basically wipe a person's identity and to do so in a way that was irretrievable by unauthorized third parties."

"In case you ever were to fall into enemy's hands…" Anne observed wistfully with a long gaze.

Jonah's eyes welled up, a single tear rolling down his cheek. "I-I still don't know what's happening. What is the Dominion? Why is this—this… thing in my head? I-I just…"

Moved with sudden compassion, Anne reached out and rested her hand on Jonah's shoulder. A moment of silence passed between them all before Ed finally spoke.

"His best bet would be returning to the Dominion."

Anne removed her hand and turned to Ed in shock. "And how the hell are we going to do that? Do you want to bring their attention here?"

"For all we know we already have it. That could be exactly why he's here."

"And you want to turn that 'could be' into a *definitely?*"

"We have to think of what's best for this man."

"What about what's best for *us?* For every member of this research community?"

"If we have to abandon the station, that might be a sacrifice we have to make. It's a matter of principles and ethics."

"Ethics and principles which the Dominion wouldn't observe on *our* behalf."

"Which is why we have to hold to them. We have to be better than that."

"And how do you know they won't just quietly bomb us out of existence before we get a chance to leave?"

"I doubt it would come to that."

"But you don't *know* that. What amount of risk would be acceptable when it's the lives of everyone here in the balance?"

"You know I've never subscribed to consequentialism. What's at stake is the wellbeing and dignity of an individual. This individual."

"Excuse me," Jonah interjected, "I don't remember much, but I still seem to recall it being generally rude to talk about someone like they're not even in the room. I'm here. I'm… I'm confused. I still don't even know where I am exactly." Tyler wiped away his tears of self-pity and shook his head.

Anne sighed.

"Talos Mystico," blurted out Ed.

"What?" Jonah asked.

"That's where you are. The name of this station. Originally, this place was constructed to study the native flora and fauna of this planet—Solus 4. But since then we've stumbled upon a number of… well, remains. Tools. Primitive pottery as best we could tell. Since then the Institute has sent us several anthropologists, another exobiologist, and one very bright-minded biochemist."

With this last remark, he glanced over at Anne before continuing. "It's a pretty notable find. In fact, the first one of its kind—at least this explicitly. And that puts us in a peculiar spot on account of this planet's position territorially speaking."

"Heh, that's putting it mildly," Anne interjected.

Ed nodded and continued. "You see, Jonah, we're outside Confederal space and the next system over is part of the Dominion. This planet is in a prime spot to be annexed."

Jonah's head was spinning now. He recognized many of the words, but their specific context eluded him. He had a fuzzy recollection of territories and political systems in the abstract, but no specific identification with Confederation or Dominion or what the ramifications of any of it really was.

"What would be so bad about being annexed? What-what is this Dominion?"

Anne spoke up, her arms folded now in irritation, her voice touched with fire, "Tyrannical despots. Self-righteous prigs. Humorless zealots with shit for brains!"

When she was done shaking her head, Anne caught Jonah staring at her with a furrowed brow of confusion. Her tone changed suddenly as her arms fell to her side. "I mean, no offense…"

"Tell us what you *really* think, Anne," Ed remarked with a smirk. Turning to Jonah, he then continued, "Anne confused your inquiry for definition with one for subjective qualitative insight." He then paused and eyed Anne as he said, "A common mistake." Turning back to Jonah he remarked, "Anne has forgotten how much you've forgot."

Anne rolled her eyes and started pacing, still visibly irritated.

Ed continued. "The Kyrian Dominion is an interstellar system of governance presided over by a council of clerics. It started as a religiously motivated political movement. When I was Kyrian I was a bit of a sympathizer myself." At this remark Anne cocked an eyebrow and glared at Ed. "Of course that was over two decades ago. My personal story is a bit, well… complicated. Anyhow, since then it evolved into a quasi-military organization until quickly a full-blown violent revolution.

"Over the span of a few short years it managed to lay claim to half a dozen planet-state systems outside the Interstellar Confederation, taking each planet by force. Of course, they would probably dispute that characterization. They would say they are simply 'raising a flag' for 'the Sovereign' and reclaiming what is The One's. They send in evangelists first. Urging the inhabitants of these outlying systems to embrace The One's *will*. And those who resist are 'handed over to Revelle.'"

"Handed over to Revelle?"

"'For the destruction of the flesh' as their holy book says."

"So is that what you—what you guys think could happen here?"

Anne remained silent, her back to them both, arms still folded. Ed sighed for a moment. "I have to admit it *is* a possibility."

"But isn't this planet big enough? Why *this* station? What did Anne mean about bombing?"

Anne turned around and spoke up. "Because our findings shatter their precious little backwards-ass worldview. Centuries ago, people couldn't have possibly descended from irrational animal ancestors. And once they lost that debate, it was 'okay, but only the once.' Only on one planet. Only with one species."

Ed nodded, "A fair summary I suppose. Rigid minds don't deal well with fluid questions. A steady stream can cut through rocks, washing away the mightiest of boulders. They say themselves that they rest their trust upon a rock. And the paradox remains that while they fear damnation, they put themselves in the business of damming up the minds of men."

"Yeah, shit for brains just like I said," Anne remarked.

Ed chuckled and shook his head. "Heh, that's one way of wording it."

"So, where does that leave me?" Jonah asked with a sullen expression. "These… people. They're the only ones who can help me?"

Another moment of silence fell, while Anne and Ed quietly contemplated. Anne then spoke up. "What about Confederation Intelligence? If anyone has an interest in cracking Jonah's br—err," she looked to Jonah "that is, disabling this inhibitor. They definitely would, right?"

"Hmm, it would be killing two birds with one stone."

"I know, right?"

"It will take several days to get a message back to the Institute. And then it could be four to six months for anyone else to arrive at this point."

"It's worth a shot, isn't it?"

They both turned and looked at Jonah, who glanced back at them with pleading, confused eyes filled with cautious trust and desperate hope.

"It is at that," Ed remarked and then repeated, "It is at that…"

THE next stop was Dr. Julia Jenkins, the station's resident medic. Anne escorted Jonah back across a series of
walkways to a structure near the tree line. Dr. Jenkins
examined him with assorted probes and instruments as Anne
explained his peculiar situation with the implant, while Jonah
sat staring out a large window looking out across the open
field beyond. Jenkins seemed to check it off in her head non-
chalantly, without much further ado. She was primarily inter-
ested in Jonah's medical history—of which they knew next to
nothing—and examining him for any pathogens. Jenkins was
a polite, but quiet and matter-of-fact kind of woman, so once
the brief exam was over she sent them on their way with a
small smile and went off to some solitary task in her private
office.

After Jenkins, Anne proceeded to give Jonah a tour of the
station and introduced him to a number of resident re-
searchers. There was the mess hall, several laboratories, a mate-

rial warehouse, apartments, and—most curiously—the aquaponic vivarium. This last locale was situated outside the interconnected web of station structures near the clearing. It was a large dome by itself, slightly elevated above the grassy ground by less than a meter. Inside was a grated walkway above large long pools. Floating on the surface of these pools were rows and rows of food crops, situated—he was told—on clear flat "rafts."

Anne explained to him as they went along how everything in the station was built to be elevated above the surrounding landscape so as to disturb the natural environment as little as possible. This is also why the vivarium was sealed with a decontamination chamber. Cross-contamination was a bilateral concern, both for the unknown effect on food production and care for the ecological impact they may have on the planet's native biosphere itself.

The only part of the complex Jonah hadn't been shown was the fusion power and sewage treatment plants. These were both on the opposite side of the station from the clearing, about half a kilometer away in the midst of another clearing.

Anne and Jonah had dinner in the modest mess hall with a couple of her colleagues. The three talked while Jonah listened quietly to largely incomprehensible conversation. As awkward as it was at times, Jonah was nevertheless grateful for the company and the food and the curious acceptance he received from the folks he had met.

In the early evening, Anne escorted Jonah to the living quarters she had arranged for him earlier. An apartment recently emptied by the departure of a senior staff member whose assignment had ended. As the door slid open, it revealed a bare undecorated interior. A simple bed along the far wall in the midst of a great empty space.

"If you need anything, I'm just right down there," Anne said as she pointed to a small treehouse structure three units down from their present location on the other side of a criss-cross walkway.

"Thank you. I really appreciate… everything."

"You're welcome," she replied with a nod and a smile.

"I certainly feel that way, yes."

"Hm," she quietly laughed. "Glad to hear it. It's… well, it's good to have a guest around here. And… I'm sorry I wasn't so welcoming before. Heh…"

"About that. I… to be honest, I've been meaning to ask you about something."

"Oh?"

"After we… well… *struggled…* what were you doing exactly? When you were on the ground, that is."

"Huh? I'm not sure I… on the ground?"

"You were… muttering? It seemed familiar, somehow. I thought maybe it might help my… memory, but then…" He sighed.

"Oh!" she exclaimed with sudden shock. Her face then flushed, and she turned her head away and chuckled nervously. "Right, right…" she said with a sigh and then continued, "Well, it was a pretty… extraordinary situation, wasn't it? And, yeah, we were both… heh… scared."

"Mm-hmm" he replied with a nod.

"I was, uh… *praying.* Heh."

"Praying?"

"Probably pretty silly," she started before catching his enthused eyes, "well, maybe not to you. I don't know. Anyhow, I was raised nominally kavist, zhurian kavist and I—I don't really know. Just… what else can you do, I guess? Heh."

"Prayer… Supplication. Intercession. I remember these words, but I… I can't remember their… significance."

"Well… I'm sure we'll get there. You'll… you'll be okay." Anne patted him on the shoulder awkwardly. "You'll… remember."

Suddenly Jonah gazed off into the distance with a glazed over expression and started to speak in a low tone as though reciting something, "When you and I met, the meeting was over very shortly, but now it is growing something as we remember it. What it will be when we remember it at the end of our days, what it makes us in all our days till then—that is the real meaning. The other is only the beginning."[1]

"Heh, what's that from?"

"I… don't know," he said and frowned.

A moment passed in silence, and Jonah felt her staring at him. When he caught her eyes, she was peering at him with a smile.

"What is it?" he asked.

She blinked and shook her head, still smiling. "Anyhow, I should get going."

"O-okay."

"I know Dr. Reed wanted to see you in the morning. And I'll meet you there tomorrow afternoon some time, after I get caught up at the lab."

"Sounds, uh, sounds good."

"Take care, Jonah."

He smiled and nodded. "You too… Anne."

After a few parting glances, he slowly turned and made his way inside. The door slid shut, and he was faced with silence. He listened to the emptiness. The space was clean. Clinically clean. It made him ill at ease.

The bed looked comfortable enough, but in some ways he preferred how he slept the night prior. Curled up by the fire. Resting against the stones. Lying upon warm earth beneath a sea of stars. Shadows of trees in the distance.

He could see a tree or two outside the window on the far wall. At least there was that. But there was something else missing in this space. Something to give it warmth. And then it came to him. Even if he were sleeping outside in the woods curled up by a fire, the trees wouldn't be life enough. Not anymore. What he really wanted now is something he hadn't known last night.

In a word, he was lonely. He hadn't missed it before, because he hadn't encountered it, save for the old man. And he mourned that stranger. But now he had gotten to tentatively know someone. At least for a few hours.

And that's when he was struck with a twinge of fear. For gain introduced the possibility of loss. If he never came to know goodness, he would never mourn its going. The thought was paralyzing. But like a spell, it broke. *'Tis better to have…* well, the word that followed might be premature to be sure. Nevertheless, he knew that to mourn was to remember. And having lost his own memory, he understood how precious a memory—even a painful one—really is.

His soft steps echoed loudly in the harsh quiet as he made his way to the bed and inspected a nearby night stand. There was a tablet lying on its surface. He picked it up and instinctively navigated its screens, tapping and swiping with his index and middle fingers.

He managed to figure out how to find a library of music accessible through an interface and play something he recognized by the title. *Fantasia on a theme.* When he selected it, music magically sounded throughout the apartment from some unseen auditory system. Lying in bed, he was bathed in waves of sound. An ocean of tremulous strings. In his mind he waltzed on those waves, casually traversing a sea of sound, quieting his stormy heart. For some reason the song inspired in him peace and hope.

As the twilight faded and night approached, he whiled away the hours listening to music and reading an assortment of literature accessible on the tablet. He finally fell asleep in

the dark, drifting into a sound sleep in the middle of an ambient melody.

IN the morning, he slowly awoke from a disquieting dream. He was running. Running in bright white snow from a big black shadow. It crept after him, clawing after him. When it finally grabbed hold of his legs, it started to drag him backward and envelop him in darkness. But then it stopped. The darkness faded away like mist, evaporating with a twinkling sound. The twinkle of bells continued as he lethargically lifted his eyelids. The room gently glowed in the golden light of dawn.

The twinkling bells was the sound of some chiming melody ringing from the tablet by his bed. When he got a proper look at the interface, it flashed the time back at him. Someone, it would seem, had set an alarm on his behalf.

After having a look around, he found a closet with some spare clothes. He then proceeded to the alcove with toilet and shower (which he already found the night prior) and made use of the facilities. After getting dressed, he promptly left the apartment with some subdued excitement. He was ready to get out of that lonely space. When he exited the front door, he took a nice long stretch and breathed in the morning air, scented as it was with the freshness of the forest. It was time to visit Dr. Reed.

"Good morning, Jonah!" Ed exclaimed with a smile.

"Good morning!"

"I hope the accommodations were good."

"Uh… yeah, yes. I'm really grateful."

"They're not much, but I imagine it's nice to sleep in a bed for a change, eh?"

"Yeah, yeah. I… yeah." Jonah coughed nervously.

"So… you're probably wondering why I asked to see you this morning."

"Uh, yeah, heh, kinda. Anne told me you wanted to see me, but not about what exactly. I… uh, I think she set an alarm for me too?"

Ed chuckled. "Sounds about right. I'm sure she'd set an alarm for me too if she could sneak into my quarters."

Jonah responded with some nervous laughter.

"Well, anyhow, it's nothing too invasive. Not going to poke and prod you like Jenkins. Just wanted to go through some assessments with you. Skills and interests. Psychometrics. Maybe a simulation or two in the system."

"Uh, o-okay."

"If you'd like to lie down, we can get started," Ed said as he gestured to the same cushioned table where he was examined the day prior.

"You… need to scan my head again?" Jonah asked with some trepidation.

"Oh, no no. Here…" Ed tapped something on a nearby console, and the cylinder-shaped scanning apparatus at the head of the table quickly lowered and retracted. A cushioned crescent shape rose in its place.

After gesturing for Jonah to lie down, Ed started to explain, "So I'm going to take you into neurospace. Just so there's no surprises, I'll outline what that means exactly…

"Neurospace is a networked virtual environment. Or, at least potentially networked. Today, I think we'll just stay local. But suffice it to say, your entire nervous system is going to be interfaced with the system. We'll do some immersion calibration to ensure the interface is working out and engage by steps."

"Is that going to, uh… hurt?"

"No, no. It totally shouldn't. If it does, let me know immediately, of course. But I don't expect any issues. The safety controls are very robust and there hasn't been a known issue for… I don't even know… decades?

"Anyhow, the interface is entirely wireless. It still requires fairly close proximity, both on account of the power requirements and regulatory reasons. Well… ethical concerns, essentially. If this system were applied at long ranges there would be —well… I'm getting off track.

"Essentially, your nervous system will be subjected to a virtual environment. It works by talking with the transceiver in your head. If you were like an average Dominionist this wouldn't work at all."

"Wouldn't work? Why?"

"The Dominion bans any neuro-interface implants. Even ones outside the cranium. Not even artificial limbs. Strictly old school prosthetics."

Jonah thought for a moment while Ed stopped to tap away on a console. Ed glanced at Jonah out of the corner of his eye, almost as if he were waiting on Jonah.

"So… if it's banned, how do I have one?"

"Ah… great question. Certainly seems duplicitous, doesn't it? But that's just one of many examples of double standards. 'Raiding the storehouses of Kemet,' they might call it. Or 'theocratic warfare' perhaps. 'Special dispensation.' Whatever the justification is it essentially amounts to permitting some personnel to bend or break the rules when it suits the purposes of advancing ecclesiastical interests, while simultaneously enforcing arbitrary dictates on the citizenry with an iron fist."

"Hmm…"

"Heh, sorry, getting off track again. Pretty soon you'll have me going on a rant like Anne."

"Anne sure was… angry."

"Don't take it personally. She understands your situation. She just has some baggage to sort through. I guess we all do on some level or other."

"I see… She was very helpful after that. I really appreciate everything—everyone here. I mean, it's been…"

Ed simply nodded in reply and then continued, "So, are you ready to try diving in?"

"S-sure, I guess."

"Alright, this may be a little disorienting at first…" Ed remarked while tapping away on the console. A low murmuring hum started to rumble. "At this point, go ahead and close your eyes."

"Okay."

"Alright, and just a moment… okay, there. Go ahead and open them now."

Jonah did as he was instructed and immediately gasped. He was in the middle of a bright blue sky. A large cloud was below and beside him. Big white puffs of moisture rolled along slowly.

"Wha-where am I?"

"You're still here. In the cybernetics lab. At this point, you still feel the table beneath you, right? That's because I've only tapped into your visual cortex to start. Feel free to have a look around."

"This-this is… amazing!"

"Hm," Ed breathed, in amusement.

"Whoa… I'm… standing?"

"Doesn't feel like it yet, does it?"

"No, it's uh… this is pretty… odd," Jonah remarked as he looked down at his virtual feet. The incongruity was starting to make him a little sick.

"So, I'll go ahead and fix that for you. How about… now?"

"Ugh… I'm getting… tingles everywhere."

"That's normal. We've moved on from the occipital lobe to the parietal lobe. You should have synchronized motor control now."

"This is so odd. Where am I? I mean… Where is this simulation? What am I standing on? It looks like fog at my feet. And I can still hear you. That humming sound is still there."

"Walking in the clouds, my friend. As far as the sound goes, we'll start talking to substructures in your temporal lobe next… Okay, there we go. Now can you still…"

"Still what…? Hello…?"

Ed's voice had faded away, along with the persistent hum and the rest of the sounds of the lab. In their place was the rushing sound of wind coming regularly in bursts, along with the sound of his own voice in the midst of an otherwise quiet open space.

"Can you hear me now?" a voice boomed from above, seemingly from the sun.

"Yes. Can you hear me…?"

"I can indeed. From the simulation, that is. Looks like you're out now, but I'll do one more test before diving in myself."

"Out now?"

"Ready for a quick drop?"

"Quick drop?"

"I just need to test your paralysis. You should have no exogenous stimuli at this point, but motor control may still need to be calibrated."

"Okay."

"Alright, this should be quick."

"Oh-kuh—ahhh!" Jonah exclaimed as the cushion of air he was standing on suddenly went away. He was in free fall. The sun and sky and approaching landscape whirled around him as he continued to fall and fall. "Gahh!"

Then it stopped. He had instinctively covered his eyes during the fall to shield them from the whirling sun. When he uncovered them, he was standing on a cloud again. A mild breeze blew past. It took a moment or two for his breathing to slow and his heart to stop pounding in his chest.

"Well, if that's not a test, what is, eh?"

It was Ed. He was now standing beside him as Jonah turned to look. He was dressed differently, but his face was much the same. Same soft smile in the middle of a short-trimmed beard.

"Ugh, what… what was that?" Jonah asked with some exasperation.

"That was supposed to be a *lot* quicker drop. Closer to half a second than half a minute. Sorry about that."

"I had no idea this would be so… immersive."

"I suppose it's one of those things that's difficult to convey without simply experiencing it. As I said, there's bound to be some disorientation at first."

Jonah nodded and had a look around. Off in the distance, he could see a peak rising from the horizon past the edge of the cloud.

"Feel like checking it out?" Ed asked.

"What?"

"That peak. It's a simulation of Mount Haku—the one here on Solus 4 that is."

"How would we get there?"

"Fly, of course."

"What do you mean? Like in a craft?"

"No, with just yourself. Ever flown in a drea—err… Right, right. Well, here, I'll show you. I'll start by hovering." With that, Ed crouched down and suddenly sprang up in the air, hopping up at least four meters. From there, with his hands stretched out below his waist as though balancing on some invisible set of beams, he stayed aloft.

Jonah simply stared in wonder.

"It all comes down to will and imagination. Imagine what it would feel like to do this and then… just… do it," Ed explained.

Jonah smiled and nodded, and then proceeded to crouch and spring himself up. To his astonishment, he shot up in the air just as Ed had, but then quickly fell back to the soft spongy floor of the cloud.

"That was pretty good. You just have to hold yourself up now. Different people take different approaches, and the program's pretty flexible. I prefer holding myself up with my hands and feet. It has to make *some* kind of sense—to you at least."

"Okay, okay. Wow…" Jonah said with a laugh and then bounced up again. This time coming to a stop as he hovered in the air next to Ed.

"Awesome. Now whenever you're ready we'll push off and jet ourselves to the mountain. Just go as fast as you can, and I'll do the same. That should keep us at the same pace."

Jonah nodded excitedly with a wide grin. "Ready when you are!"

They flew breathlessly fast. Almost literally, with the rush of wind whooshing by at their sky-streaking pace. It was only a matter of moments before the mountain peak came rushing up toward them, and following Ed's cue, they whipped around and slowed their descent with their hands and feet. They both gently touched down like a whisper on the mountaintop.

"Good. Very good," Ed remarked with a smile.

"Heh, thanks."

"I wouldn't doubt if you've done this before."

"Really?"

"Yeah, I think so. The only thing locked away in that cranium of yours is memory effectively related to your personal identity. There's bound to be a lot of talent and skill just waiting to be discovered."

"Huh…" Jonah said with a dash of awe. For some reason, he hadn't thought of that exactly.

"So how about we see what else you might know, eh?"

"Okay…"

"System register voice control, user jay-cee."

"Jay-cee?" Jonah asked. As he did another voice emanated from the surrounding air. A soft feminine voice lilting on the wind in all directions.

"User registered. Voice controls unlocked."

"You're all set," Ed said. "Care to reset the environment?"

"Reset…? H-how…?"

"Do you perhaps… recall?"

Jonah looked down for a moment with furrowed brow. Then, relaxing, suddenly looked up with wide eyes of realization. "System load constructor canvas."

The world around them disintegrated. The mountain. The sky. All was replaced with a large white cube of a room.

"Excellent!" Ed exclaimed.

Jonah looked around in awe, then shot a glance back at Ed and laughed.

"Alright, Jonah. How about we figure out what else you know how to do, eh…?"

SEVERAL hours passed. Ed had Jonah perform a number of tasks. He asked him to identify and operate assorted pieces of technology, solve an assortment of puzzles, and even had him sit down for half an hour or so with a virtual "counselor" in a cozy, warm-lit office. Jonah generally enjoyed the diverse set of experiences, although he wasn't always sure what Ed wanted from the whole thing precisely. It was a comprehensive examination process, but all for what exactly? In any case, he hadn't noticed the time go by when Ed finally suggested they get back to the "real world" for a bit and have some lunch.

When they arrived at the mess hall, Jonah looked around for Anne, but she was nowhere to be found. He was quickly distracted, however, by Ed's sudden excited exclamation.

"All right! Nipponese curry and rice! I love Nipponese curry!"

"Curry?" Jonah asked.

"Yeah, it's the best. Get it while it's hot, man."

It didn't look terribly appetizing to him, but Jonah shrugged his shoulders and spooned some rice on to his dish and poured the curry over it, carefully imitating Ed. It didn't smell awful, but he was a tad skeptical about the strange brown chunky sauce.

They sat down in the sparsely crowded room next to a dark-skinned woman quietly picking at a mostly empty bowl of rice, as she perused a nearby tablet.

"Abebe! You didn't get the curry?" Ed asked with a touch of bewilderment.

"A bay bay…" Jonah mouthed to himself quietly.

"Heh, no. Stir-fry," the woman responded, still scrolling on the device.

"Oh man! You're missing out!"

"I'm not a man and I prefer the stir fry," she said, glancing up at Ed momentarily before returning her eyes to the device.

"Suit yourself, Aisha. But you're seriously missing out. Julio outdid himself this time." Ed then perched up slightly and called out to an olive skinned man behind the nearby counter. "Hey, Julio! You really outdid yourself this time, amigo!"

The bronze-brown man smiled and nodded with a slow blink. The woman across from Ed with the mocha complexion chortled quietly at the exchange, while continuing to keep her eyes fixed on the tablet.

"Oh, hey, have you met my friend Jonah here?"

She looked up with a soft smile. "I can't say that I have."

"Jonah, this is Dr. Abebe. Dr. Abebe, allow me to introduce you to Mister Jonah Tyler."

"Thank you, Doctor Reed," she said as she reached out her hand to Jonah. "Pleasure to meet you, Mister Tyler."

"Okay, now dig in, man!" Ed exclaimed to Jonah.

Jonah gave a small nervous smirk to them both and proceeded to scoop up half a spoon full of curry and rice. He then cautiously spooned it in his moth and slowly tasted it. It tasted… pretty good, actually. He took a bigger scoop and gulped it down. Very good, in fact.

"Mm!" Jonah exclaimed unconsciously.

"Really good, right?"

Jonah nodded enthusiastically. He hadn't tasted anything quite like it. At least, of course, that he could remember. Smooth, yet spicy. The deliciously complex herbs harmoniously complimented the subtle simplicity of the starchy potato chunks and white sticky rice.

"Julio told me yesterday they were expecting a fresh harvest of potatoes from the vivarium. And, *man*, he did not disappoint."

"So, Ed, are you going to be in neuro later today?" Dr. Abebe asked.

"Probably not. Already spent over four hours today. I don't want Jenkins breathing down my neck about it."

"Alright, I'll just ping you about it then. I wanted to get your take on some heuristics later. I'm planning on integrating them into that subsystem we discussed yesterday."

"Sure thing. I'll review and shoot you over some annotations."

"Thanks. Well, gentlemen, I should be on my way. Pleasure meeting you, Mister Tyler." After a quick exchange of nods and polite smiles, she left.

There was a short ensuing silence filled only with the distant sounds of clattering dishes, chewing, and occasional enthusiastic grunts from Ed as the two continued to eat. When Jonah was about halfway through his dish, he spoke up.

"So…"

"Hm?"

"You, uh, said you used to be Kyrian…?"

"Heh…" Ed coughed with some barely detectable embarrassment, followed by a momentary reflective pause. "Yes… used to be."

"So what was it like? You said you were in the Dominion?"

"No, no. I was never in the Dominion. I, uh… *sympathized*—to my present chagrin—but I was never actually a 'citizen of the Sovereign' as they say."

"Oh…"

"Like I said, my story is a little complicated."

Another moment of silence passed as they continued eating, before Jonah spoke up again.

"You could, uh, tell it if you wanted."

"Oh, well…" he started with a sigh. "Where would I start?"

"The beginning's fine," Jonah remarked with a smile.

"Heh, no better place to start I suppose, eh? Okay, well…" Ed said and paused, reflecting. "I was born and raised on Aridus 2—a mining colony just a handful of parsecs from Helios 3, although it didn't feel like it at the time. I was under a massive shared dome with a million or so fellow inhabitants, but my family and I might as well have been on another world all together.

"I was born and raised in a fundamentalist sect. The Saints of Elwayae. Growing up was a little strange. No birthdays or holidays of any kind. Everybody seems to know that one. Refusing treats when they were part of celebrations at the school where I went. But I guess what most people don't necessarily know about is the half a dozen gatherings a week. Tedious study sessions that drag on for hours into the night. Or how leaving merits institutional shunning. Friends and family torn apart when someone commits some grievous transgression—which could include something as simple as expressing disagreement with doctrine. That one, in fact, merits the most severe punishment.

"And that's the one I ultimately did. My sister hasn't spoken to me in almost a couple decades now. Heh."

"Wh-what? I'm not sure I understand. She doesn't talk to you at all?" Jonah asked in a bit of shock.

"Apostasy isn't tolerated amongst the Saints. An alderman actually told a friend of mine at the time when I was leaving that 'I absolutely do hate him, just as Elwayae does.' They wish death upon apostates, and if they had political power they, would execute them. Since they don't, they do the next best—or worst—thing and treat them as *though* they're dead. And that's effectively how my sister treats me."

"That's terrible…"

"It is what it is," Ed said with a shrug. "Anyhow, a lot more could be said about all that, but it's old news at this point, and not perfectly relevant to what you want to know I'm sure.

"I just accepted the way I was raised, because I was raised in it. We accept the reality which we're presented. I accepted mine. It was the only world I knew.

"But when that changed one day—slowly, progressively, and then with a sudden shock—I was thrown into a flux. It was like awakening in the midst of some dark wreckage. Everything I knew thrown in shambles. And then slowly climbing out of the dark, like emerging from a cave. And then trying to let my eyes adjust to the brightness outside before I could make sense of anything. I don't know if any of that makes sense to you."

"I think it… does…" Jonah replied, staring off into the distance reflectively.

"Well, suffice it to say, in a state like that you try to hold on to what makes sense. You cling to things. The things that might still make sense to you. You hold on to them like treasured possessions. Even some things that seem useless now. You can't help but hold on to everything.

"Later when you start to acquire an abundance you can start to let some of those things go. Really evaluate what you actually need or could make use of. Know what I mean?"

Jonah nodded enthusiastically. He wasn't sure precisely what Ed was getting at, but he could completely relate, curiously enough, on an emotional level at the very least.

"So, suffice it to say over the course of a few months I came to have left one fringe sect of Kyrianism to come to embrace something of the more mainstream variety. I styled myself something of an Infralapsarian Hobbsian, heh. One who subscribed to Preterism and Unigenic Evolution. Well, the latter came a little later. For a while I was more of a Progressive —well…" Ed stopped himself and chuckled. "I'm sure little of these words make sense to you at this point."

"Hmm…" Jonah thought for a moment. "A few of them seem strangely familiar, but… I can't… quite… recall."

"Right. Well, I'm pretty certain at this point I have a good idea of your background, and how intrinsic some of these concepts would be to your prior identity. Unfortunately, that's precisely why they would be suppressed by the inhibitor."

Jonah sighed and frowned.

Ed responded with a reassuring voice. "Something, uh… I'm sure could very likely be rectified in a matter of months."

"Really?"

"Yes, I think so. I sent out a message to the Institute last night. Once they receive it, I'm sure a number of folks with the State will read it with great interest," Ed explained with a measure of somber hope.

Jonah nodded and smirked, feeling a little sorry for himself, but also feeling some reassurance. Ed in turn gazed off to the side in thought, staring with a twinge of melancholy that went unnoticed.

"So you were saying you *sympathized* with the Dominion?"

Ed continued with a sigh, "Right, yeah. Well… in my defense back then it was largely civil. A political movement within the Confederation to reform society through peaceful means and bring it more in line with… heh… Kyrian values.

"But over time I came to saw the toxicity of the perspective it promoted and perpetuated. In fact, it's part of what made me rethink my own Kyrianism."

"Oh?"

"Not directly. But… well… ultimately the fundamental message—the central claim—of Kyrianism is rooted in supposedly historic events that we only know about through the Kyrio. And if we come to realize how utterly fallible the *contemporary* Kyrio is—prone to all manner of cognitive bias and tribalism—then how can we trust the *ancient* Kyrio? Men and women—heh, well, mostly men—who were even *more* subject to bias and tribalism in a pre-scientific age.

"When I saw respectable, otherwise thoughtful men— thinkers and leaders within the community—come to proliferate some of the most unsubstantiated nonsense… well… suffice it to say it gave me pause. And so I reconsidered old lines of reasoning and the evidence I once came to accept, and, in short, found it wanting to say the least."

"I *think* I understand. You stopped agreeing with this 'Kyrianism' because other people were lying. Something like that?"

"No, not exactly. It's simply a matter that, well… it's incredibly difficult to tell the truth. There is such a thing as *intellectual* dishonesty. And that's something that can creep in on any one of us if we're not careful. It takes a profound amount of humility, self-awareness, and conscious effort to actually seek out truth and continue to re-evaluate what we believe.

"So, it's not as though the folks I knew were actively looking to deceive anyone. From their perspective, they fervently believe what they preach and teach, as far as I can tell. But if I'm honest with myself, and listen to my own conscience—a point on which I think they and I would still agree —I cannot call myself a Kyrian or uphold its claims. But, yeah, there's a lot more I could say on the subject to be sure."

"Heh, I'm starting to get that impression."

"Talking the new guy's ear off, Ed?" Julio called out from the counter.

"Hey, it's not very often we get someone new around here. And this guy isn't a know-it-all like us PhDs."

Julio and Ed shared a chuckle before Julio continued. "Where's he from anyhow? I saw him in here yesterday with Anne, but I didn't think we had any new arrivals coming."

"Anne didn't introduce you to Mister Tyler?"

"I have to say I was very busy at the time, Dr. Reed," Julio explained and then waved to Jonah. "Nice to meet you, Señor Tyler."

"Nice to meet you," Jonah replied with a smile and wave.

"So did you ship in from Helios 3?" Julio asked.

"Oh, uh…" Jonah stuttered.

"It's a little… complicated." Ed started to explain. "We actually pulled Jonah in here as an emergency assist. He's not staffed with the project."

"Oh?" Julio asked with a furrowed brow. "If he's not staff, then…"

"Apparently, I'm, uh… from the Dominion?"

"Ay, mi Sobreano!" Julio exclaimed with a gasp as his eyes widened.

"He's been vetted," Ed immediately retorted, holding up a hand reassuringly. "Jonah here has been suffering some memory loss. Dr. Ericson is aware of the situation."

Julio responded by blowing out his breath and shaking his head. "I guess you guys know what you're doing. I'm just the cook. Ay yai yai."

"You're too modest, man." Ed replied. And then turning to Jonah while pointing at Julio with his thumb remarked "Best chef in the galaxy. No joke." Then turning back to Julio, "How many culinary awards do you have again, Julio?"

"Awards don't pay the bills, my friend. You guys get the big bucks."

"Right, because we all know research grants are a sure path to a life of luxury. I can't wait to get back to my private starship."

The two laughed, and Jonah chuckled along with them.

"Alright, well, I'll see you later muchacho," Julio said with a smile, and then with his grin ever so slightly fading away he turned to Jonah and waved. "Nice to, uh, meet you, Señor Tyler."

Jonah nodded and coughed nervously.

W HEN Ed and Jonah returned to the office, Ed asked Jonah to assist him with a number of tasks, and Jonah was happy to oblige. As part of Ed's earlier assessments, it turned out Jonah had some acquaintance with writing network configuration scripts. Ed showed Jonah how to operate the music catalog on his screen and gave him two tracking stickers to apply to the outside of his tragus on each ear. They spent the afternoon working independently in relative silence, each absorbed in their own audiovisual bubbles.

Initially, Jonah wondered why they couldn't just go back to neurospace. Just thinking of his experience there was exhilarating. But as Ed explained, the station's resident medic had set strict guidelines for neurospace usage. It was strongly advised that no one spend more than 30 hours in a given week, and that included both work and recreation. And so they did their work out in the real world of the office interior, in between a break or two including an occasional walk outdoors—another piece of medical advice they were strongly urged to follow.

After a few hours, a chime came at the door. It was Anne.

"Hey guys!" she said when Ed opened the door. Jonah turned in his chair and gave a small smile and wave as she entered.

"Long time no see. What do they have you examining today? Stool samples?"

"Heh, I wish," she said without a hint of irony. "Something so overt would be quite a find. We did manage to come across some intriguing organic residue on one of the flint tool artifacts. It's definitely recent, but it's hard to say how it got there precisely."

"Well, here's hoping you have a shitty day tomorrow."

Anne replied with a chuckle, a small shake of the head, and a quick eye roll. Jonah noted how her hair glittered as it bounced in the light of the late afternoon. In the glow of some far off beam shining through the canopy, her hair was really almost auburn. Most of it was tied back in a ponytail, with a single delicate lock drifting down the side of her pale gold face. A face punctuated by two gleaming emerald eyes. Eyes which he suddenly realized were staring back at him now.

"Ed making you do his homework?" she said, gesturing to the screen behind him with a nod.

"Huh? Uh…" Jonah replied as he turned back in his chair awkwardly.

"Hey, somebody's gotta work around here," Ed remarked.

"I know, and it's not going to be you anytime soon," Anne replied with a snicker.

"Exactly!" Ed exclaimed with a chuckle.

"So seriously, did you get word back from the director?" Anne asked, lowering her voice a little.

"Yeah, yeah, I did," Ed replied with a sober nod.

"How did the assessment turn out?" Anne asked, glancing briefly at Jonah.

"Swimmingly. And actually, it looks like Jonah has a distinct set of skills that should prove useful here."

"Where's here exactly?"

"*Here*, here. In my lab. He has a knack for information systems and cryptography. Something not entirely unexpected, of course."

"Hmm," Anne replied with a nod.

Ed approached closer and spoke more discretely, "And, uh, this goes well enough with my thoughts on mitigation…"

"Hopefully it doesn't come to that," Anne replied in a hushed tone.

"Either way, I think it's a good idea, purely for the, uh, subject's sake. Even… within… custody, it would be a rude awakening. Our best shot is to have an ally—a willing one."

Anne nodded somberly. Her eyebrows then shot up with a flash of thought. "Oh, did you hear about the sighting last night?"

"No, I hadn't. Sighting?"

"Yeah, possibly another ship. Hard to pinpoint its location, but the report seemed to indicate it was seen hovering somewhere south of the basin near Wellington Falls."

"I'm guessing Frank is going to check it out then."

"It already left, but yeah, Frank is going to check out the area anyhow."

"So…" Jonah interjected with some measure of discomfort, "Should I just, uh, come back here tomorrow?"

Ed turned to Jonah with a smile, "That's up to you, man. I could definitely use the help if you'd like."

"Uh, yeah, I mean… this has been all pretty interesting. You really could use the help?"

"Jonah, I have a feeling we could all use your help more than you know."

With that, Jonah laughed a little awkwardly, detecting some manner of subtext but unsure of its nature. Nearby, Anne nodded somberly as she gazed off into space.

After they parted ways for the night with an exchange of handshakes, Jonah headed back to his apartment and looked off toward Anne as she glided back to her own domicile. He watched as she approached her door in the distance and waved when he saw her face turn toward his. She gave a quick wave back and a smirk before heading in.

He was faced with the emptiness of his private sanctuary again, but this time he was met with a sense of hope and expectation as well. The third day of his short life was over, but he couldn't help feel that, with tomorrow's dawn, something new was about to begin.

THREE weeks passed. At least by the standard interstellar calendar. The day-night cycle on Solus 4 was roughly 24 hours, but there was no moon and thus no phases to lend the seven days of a week any local significance. But then it had been a long time since people were enchanted by the moon. Luna had been forsaken as men sought after other stars.

Jonah had been learning this history for days now. Philosophy, religion, science, and art. Ed had made all manner of reading suggestions and took an hour or two every day to give Jonah a rambling lecture. As Ed had told him, "While I can't tell you much about your personal past, I can tell you about the past we all share."

Jonah made for a very enthusiastic student. Ed noted how his mind seemed to soak up everything like a sponge, uncluttered as it was from the constraints that came with most men of Jonah's age. The daily distractions of adult concerns to which so many lend more importance than they likely deserve. The lingering ghosts of the past that haunt men with self-doubt and self-absorption. And the vanity and pride that get in the way of any education. Jonah was a bit of a blank slate, but in the best of ways.

"So, what do you think?" Jonah asked with a wide grin.

"Wow… I'm seriously impressed. Very well done," Ed replied as he looked around the expansive domed interior.

They were standing in the open space of an ornately tiled hall, enclosed by two fences of columns to either side jutting out from nearby walls. Streams of sunlight came through a remote aperture in the domed ceiling of the interior. Clouds of incense wafted from a statue in the distance. Beyond the columns were stone walls in which were carved long lines of stone shelves.

"Let me show you the best part," Jonah said and gestured for Ed to follow.

He led him to one of the shelves. It was filled from end to end with books. Old medieval-style leather-bound volumes of assorted sizes set side by side. Jonah grabbed one particular tome and handed it to Ed.

"Intricate detail. Nicely designed. But…"

"But what?" Jonah asked.

"These books don't really match the period, do they? Some of the earliest codices had barely come into use by the time the Museum of Rakodia was already gone. And even an ancient codex would have used papyrus rather than parchment."

"I took some creative liberties," Jonah replied with a shrug. "Take a look inside."

Ed carefully turned back the cover and slowly flipped through the pages. He then started to snicker and then chuckle. "This… this is my thesis."

"Pretty cool, eh?"

"Heh, yeah. But… my thesis was a multimedia paper. What did you do about the embedded video?"

"Flip to page forty-two," Jonah replied with a knowing smirk.

Ed did as Jonah instructed, and as soon as he turned to page 40 a video frame grew up out of the page from trailing lines of light, as though it were being projected from the page itself. An animated diagram of a brain whirled around in the air as Ed's own voice narrated. Ed cringed a little at the sound of his voice and quickly closed the book, the video frame retreating into the page as he did.

"What do you think?" Jonah asked.

"Terrible voice narration aside, it's all *very* well done. So all of these books…?"

"Converted from the files in our document repository. Well… most of them. I have a few blank books in there for filler, but eventually we could convert all the documents. I think the interface could be as practical as it is enjoyable."

"Hmm… normally I'd say that I'm not a big fan of skeuomorphic design, but this… this takes it to another level. I'm truly impressed."

Jonah beamed with pride after Ed's remarks. Ed proceeded to then raise the back of the book to his nose and breathed in a bit, turning the book over as he gave it a whiff.

"One little detail that's kind of odd here."

"Oh?" Jonah asked with furrowed brow.

"It smells like a contemporary collegiate textbook," Ed remarked with a snicker.

"What do you mean? It's a book."

"Yeah, and different kinds of books have different smells. A dusty old parchment-based tome like this shouldn't smell of glossy paper and glue."

"Oh, huh…" Jonah replied with a frown.

"We'll have to get you a few assorted books for reference."

"Yeah," Jonah replied with a nod. "When do you think that might happen, anyways?"

"Oh, well…" Ed said with a sigh. "The last message I received back from the Institute conveyed a lot of interest. I have no doubt you'll be added to the next rotation. You'd be returning to Confederation space with the rest of us."

"How long is that again?"

"Five months and two days from this morning."

Their attention was drawn to footsteps. A click-clack of heeled boots echoed throughout the empty chamber as the silhouette of some distant figure approached from the direction of the statue. Veiled in the fog of incense and the gloom of an approaching twilight, the figure slowly made its way across the tiled floor as Jonah and Ed stared with idle curiosity.

"Hey guys!" a woman called out as she clopped along toward them. She stopped in the column of light in the center of the room and waved. In the midst of that light, her entire form was revealed. A long braided lock of white gold hair rested on a silver armored pauldron. Sharp doe-shaped ears framed a pale face with blue eyes.

"Anne? Is that you?" Ed asked, betraying a bit of amusement in his voice.

"Oh, right," the woman said as she looked down at herself. "I got roped into a session of Mists of E'davlan last night with Frank and Sumi. I haven't been in the system since then and forgot to reset my avatar, heh."

Ed chuckled as Jonah looked on with a quiet smile.

"I look like I would fit in with this place," Anne continued as she examined her surroundings. "Where are we? Frank would love this."

"It's the Museum of Rakodia," Jonah explained. "Specifically the great library portion of it. It's not intended to be a perfect replica. I mean, not that we would really be able to do that very well anyhow. I took a number of creative liberties."

"*You* built this?" Anne asked in wonder as she continued gazing at her surroundings.

"Well, I mean, I reworked some assets from an existing package. The columns are mostly default. But, I mean, yeah," Jonah said with a shrug.

"You haven't seen the best part," Ed remarked. "Come check out these books!"

"Alright," Anne agreed as she marched closer in her clip-clopping boots.

Ed picked out a tome at random and handed it to Anne. She carefully peeled back the cover before reading aloud.

"Talos Mystico Site Survey Twenty-One, heh."

"Turn the page," Ed prompted.

When Anne complied, a video frame popped up out of the page and started playing. It was aerial footage of a hill top surrounded by trees. At the top of the hill was a clearing, and in the midst of the clearing was a circle of carefully arranged boulders at regular intervals.

"Stonehenge site. Wow. This is Frank's report," Anne remarked with quiet wonder.

"Pretty clever, isn't it?" Ed asked.

"Indeed it is," Anne replied before looking up to Jonah. "You came up with this?"

Jonah nodded. "I built out a conversion algorithm and fed a sampling from our document repository through it. I thought it might be fun—and, uh, practical. Heh."

"Yeah, this is—this is pretty cool. Huh…"

"Heh, thanks."

"How much time did all this take?"

"Time—hey!" Ed interjected. "What time is it?"

"It was around eighteen local when I dropped in," Anne replied.

"Shoot, I should log off before Jenkins gets on my case."

"Hey, before you do," Anne said, "I was wondering if I could get your take on something real quick."

"Sure, what d'ya got?"

"System, instance diagram buffer, location right index fingertip," Anne called out to the air as she pointed an extended finger at eye level. As soon as she uttered "tip" a translucent figure of a bundled up molecule chain appeared in the air.

"What is that? A chromosome? Kind of outside of my area of expertise here."

"You tell me. It sure looks like one, doesn't it? And we found it in what we thought was an organism."

"What you *thought* was an organism?"

"Biofilters at the supply dock detected a fairy wasp. It got zapped into stasis."

"A fairy wasp? I'm still not following…"

"Fairy wasps are strictly native to Solidus. It's one of the numerous species of insect we screen for at the supply dock. When a supply ship isn't coupled with the dock, the filters automatically zap into stasis for later review. During docking, the filters would disintegrate anything resembling solidial life smaller than a millimeter."

"Okay…"

"Right, so anyways, the point is… inside of this apparent insect's cells, we discovered something. Silicon."

"Wait, what?"

"Exactly. So what I wanted to get your take on was this…" Anne reached out her hands and performed a stretching gesture, making the floating model expand in the process. "This strange filament structure. Can you make anything of that?"

Ed stared at the model for a moment with furrowed brow, before his jaw slowly dropped. "It's a micro-antenna."

Anne replied with a nod.

"Can you send me all the material you have on this thing?"

"You got it. First thing in the morning. In the meantime, I'll let you guys go."

"Sure thing, Anne. I definitely want to talk to you about this tomorrow."

"Talk to you then," Anne said with a wave, before disappearing before their eyes.

"So…" Ed turned to Jonah with a smirk. "Is that your muse?" he asked, gesturing to the statue on the far wall.

"It's *a* muse… why?"

"Oh, just curious. Interesting choice with the eyes…" Ed remarked as he pointed at the literal emeralds embedded in the statue's head. It was a woman with long flowing hair, hands to the side, head craned back, accentuating her bust.

"Not sure what you mean," Jonah replied, feigning ignorance.

"Just a piece of unsolicited advice… Don't get her confused with yourself."

"Huh?" Jonah replied with genuine bewilderment.

"It's easy to place an idol on a pedestal. A person, on the other hand, won't stay up there very long. They'll get tired and fall off. That's assuming they're not wise enough to knock the pedestal down as soon as they see it erected. It's incompatible with freedom, and if there's one thing people long for more than perfection, it's freedom."

"I'm not sure, I—"

"Why don't you just ask her out?"

"What?"

"Don't play dumb with me, Jonah. We both know how smart you actually are."

Jonah looked off to the side and scratched the back of his head awkwardly. He was glad the increasingly gloomy interior hid his flushed cheeks.

"I… I'm not sure… how. I mean…"

"It's simple, man. You ask if she'd like to go on a date. You make your intentions clear upfront. Radical honesty."

"But…"

"Heh…" Ed started to laugh, seeing the terror in his friend's eyes. "The scales of Leviathan shimmer as precious jewels and make a fine prize for any who might slay him. Courage. That's all it takes."

"One of these days, I'm going to get your references," Jonah said and sighed.

"I'll break this one down for you. You—like most men—are completely terrified of rejection. And why shouldn't you be? It's a dragon that seeks to devour your self-worth. The looming threat of rejection is a threat of judgment. A judgment on your intrinsic value—right down to your genes.

"You have to conquer this fear. You have to rest assured that you have value and worth. Something to really offer someone—even when that isn't everyone. It can't be everyone. And if they're not willing to receive what you're offering, you have to accept that. It's basic respect. You move on and find someone who will recognize and appreciate what you're offering.

"And when you get to that point, when you face your fear and move past it, assured and confident in your own merit, you'll be giving it the best shot you can at improving your chances of success. There's no guarantees, but accepting whatever may come—hoping for the best while planning for the worst—that's the best you can do. Does that make sense?"

"Yeah… yeah, I think so."

"So, first things first, you need to kill your gods."

"Eh?"

"This isn't a real person and never will be," Ed explained, gesturing to the statue. "Real men and women have blemishes and frailties. They're not made of stone. They're smelly fleshy bags of fears and insecurities. Doubts and ignorance. Flaws of every kind, both inside and out. And these things remind us of their reality. And reality will always be more beautiful than any facsimile. Ideals are idols when we worship *them* instead of the world as it is."

"Heh, I… yeah, I get it," Jonah said with a blushing smile.

"Speaking of reality, maybe it's about time we get back to it, eh?"

Jonah nodded. "Yeah, I guess so. Thanks, Dr. Reed."

"C'mon, man, call me Ed."

"Yeah, okay okay. Thanks again… Ed."

"Good night, Jonah."

"You too," Jonah said with a wave.

RIFTING backwards to his actual position. Tingling all over his body. Waiting for a moment of intermittent darkness to fade away. Jonah wasn't sure if he would ever become perfectly comfortable exiting neurospace. When he did, he found he was staring at the ceiling of his apartment. He rose from the reclined cushioned platform as soon as the rollers and nodes ceased massaging his limbs and back.

He knew what he wanted to do now. What he *had* to do. And he wanted to do it as soon as possible. It was a burden weighing on his mind that he wanted to shrug off, since he knew that relief would come when he did—regardless of the outcome.

He paced across the length and width of his domicile. Back and forth. All around. He needed to sort it out in his mind. What he was going to say, specifically. How he was going to say it, specifically. How he was going to be, specifically.

It was close to an hour of pacing, drinking a glass of water, eating an occasional snack, sitting down for the briefest of pauses only to jitter his feet and hop up again. Finally, he worked up the nerve, the resolve, to do it. He remembered that there was no time like the present, and came to the conclusion that he could never have it all figured out to the point of perfection. Ed was right. Freedom was more valuable than perfection, as evidenced by his own inclinations. For in the end, he longed to be free of this burden.

And so he set out from the little cage he had been pacing like a lion and set out to her apartment. It was a short stroll to her front door. His heart was racing. It was fear after all that he faced. And when he had that clear in his mind, it became easier. It's always easier to slay monsters when they can be clearly seen.

He shone a light on his soul and could see the fear trying to hide away in the dark. It tried to lie about its name. It called itself foolishness, triviality. Just a tiny bit of nonsense. A waste of time. But when he admitted to himself that what he feared was no small bit of awkwardness but rather the raging jaws of death itself—the death of his genetic line and any meaning and purpose his life may have had—then he could fight that fear sufficiently. He could give himself the assurance at which Ed had hinted. He could still have hope and move on. There was more opportunity in the future as long as the future remained. And as he grew bigger and brighter in this way, the lying little monster hiding in the dark grew smaller.

He activated her door chime. And then he waited. More than a minute passed as his heart pounded. No response. Should it really take her this long? He didn't hear the faintest hint of sound.

And that's when he heard a voice from behind.

"Jonah?" she called out inquisitively.

"Uh… h-hi, Anne—I mean Dr. Chin—err, uh…" Jonah said as he whipped around. He was caught off-guard, to say the least.

"Heh, hi. Did you, uh, need something?"

"Yes—I mean no. I mean…" Jonah said with a sigh.

"What is it?"

Jonah took a breath and blinked slowly. "I'm sorry, I just, uh…"

"Yes?"

No time like the present. He took a deep calming breath and laughed at himself a little on the inside. "I was wondering if you wanted to go out some time."

"Out? Out where?"

"Just you and me. A… a date, essentially. I, uh… Yeah. I like you, and I thought maybe we could… get to know one another better. Well, mostly you. I'm sure you know more about me and all, heh. But, uh, there—there it is. Yeah."

"Oh… uh…" Anne said, clearly surprised. She darted her eyes back and forth and laughed a little. A piercing bit of laughter that cut into Jonah, while he tried to remain calm.

"Hey, y'know, I'm sorry if I made you uncomfortable and all. Maybe it's just—yeah, it's probably kind of, I mean you probably wouldn't… uh…"

"Sure," Anne said with a nod and a smile.

"I see, sure, yeah it's okay. Sorry to bother you," Jonah said as he started to back away from her door.

"Jonah…"

"Huh?"

"I meant… sure, yeah, we could… we could do that."

"R-really?"

"Yeah, what did you have in mind?"

"O-oh, just, uh… something, y'know, casual. Just going out… somewhere."

"When?"

"Right! Right, right. Sorry, heh. Um, I was thinking maybe in the afternoon a couple days from now this weekend?"

Anne glanced off to the side and nodded her head. "Okay."

"I'll just meet you back here at your place around, say, sixteen hundred?"

"Yeah, okay. Sure."

"Great! It's, uh, it's a date!"

Anne nodded.

"It *is* a date, right?"

Anne nodded again and gave him a wide laughing grin.

"Okay, cool. I'll, uh, I'll see you then."

"Sounds like a plan."

"Yeah, cool, cool. Uh… have a good night then."

"You too, Jonah."

Jonah waved as he walked away, smiling. It took a modicum of effort not to skip away. When he got back to his apartment to the safety of indoors, he waited until the door slid shut.

"Yes!" Jonah shouted.

It took a while to get to sleep that night, but when he did, he slipped into slumber with a smile.

THE days crawled along like a tortoise with the world on its back. Ed encouraged Jonah to focus on his work and let go of the burden he was borrowing. But that was easier said than done. Some burdens are easier to carry than shrug off.

The day finally came. The last day of the calendar week. A day of rest that for Jonah seemed restless. He awoke with a mixture of anxiety and anticipation in a copper colored morning. The day's light was filtered through a cloudy haze left over from yesterday's passing rain showers. He felt a touch of melancholy that was hard to pinpoint. A general sense of discomfort somewhere just below his heart. An uneasiness in his spleen.

But his heart was set at ease with the golden light of the sun overtaking the morning clouds. As he left his apartment and breathed in the crisp morning aroma of pine—the dust dampened down by the night's drizzle—his spirit was lifted by the prospect of possibilities the day might bring. For that moment, it was as though tomorrow was already there. It was a tangible thing he could touch with his eyes in that golden light.

He spent an hour making some last minute preparations. He double-checked with Frank that he still had the clearance he needed. He double-checked with Julio that his request was still in the system and to confirm times. Both reassured him and shook their heads behind his back with silent laughing smirks.

Once he was done, it was time for more waiting. And so he did. He waited. And waited. And then waited some more. He did calisthenics for an hour or two on the forest floor, making use of some low-lying branches. He ran a few laps around the station. He even circled the power station a few times.

When it came time for lunch, he ate alone in the mess hall. He was tempted to check in with Julio again, but Julio already anticipated this. While Jonah started to scan the counter, Julio caught his eyes and gave him a nod and a thumbs up before turning his back and secretly rolling his eyes.

"Good afternoon," Jonah said when Anne answered the door.

"Oh, hi…" Anne replied with an awkward chortle.

"Oh, sorry, did I—did you, uh…"

"No, no, I'm ready to go. I just didn't realize, uh… maybe I'm not ready enough?" Anne asked as she looked down at her simple jumpsuit. It contrasted fairly sharply with Jonah's semiformal silken shirt and dress pants.

"No no, you look great. Maybe I'm actually a little over-dressed, heh…"

"Not at all. Sorry, it's just… it's been a while. I don't know what I was thinking."

"Well, it seems like it's been forever for me," Jonah said with a wry smile.

It took her a beat or two, but when she got it, Anne erupted with laughter. Her awkwardness mixed with the sudden surprise of his ironic remark worked to effect in her an explosion of hysterical convulsions. Jonah in turn was moved to a bit of gleeful giggling himself, with a wide smile and blushed face.

Once they both recovered, Jonah asked, "Shall we go then?"

"Sure, sure," Anne said with a wide grin, "W-where are we going again?"

"You'll see!"

Jonah led her along the bridging walkways between the trees to a descending platform, which they took down to the forest floor. From there he led her out to the clearing by the vivarium and marched on up to a waiting craft with its hatch already lowered.

"Wait… are you planning on flying one of the 'ropters?"

"I'm hyperopter-certified!" Jonah called back as he climbed the steps and made his way inside.

A beat or two passed as she stood still. Jonah's head perched back out of the craft. "Are you coming?"

"Heh…" she remarked to herself in disbelief, before sauntering toward the craft.

When she climbed inside, Jonah was already at the helm, starting to work the controls.

"This is Tango Delta Two checking in. Am I clear for takeoff?" Jonah asked aloud.

"Roger, Tango Delta Two. Since you're the only one with a flight plan today, you're all set," a man replied with a smirk in his voice.

"Frank?" Anne asked with surprise.

"Tango Delta Two, it sounds like I'm getting some interference on the line. Could you repeat the question? Sounded like your balls fell off or something."

"You knew about this, Frank?" Anne asked, ignoring Frank's playful vulgarity.

"I'm the one who administered his flight certification, so… yeah?"

"Heh…" Anne replied. She was quite literally dumbfounded.

"I am starting my ascent now. Tango Delta Two over and out."

"Roger roger, Tango Delta Two. You are go for launch. Ready ignition. Over and out."

"Go for launch…" Anne whispered to herself and snickered.

Jonah tapped away at a screen and the hatch door closed. He then turned to Anne with a smile. "You might want to buckle up."

The ascent was a rapid but smooth one, and Jonah handled the controls expertly. Anne watched him pilot the craft for some time before asking about how he managed to get certified. As Jonah explained, he had discovered he was capable of piloting small crafts while during his assessment with Ed weeks ago. Since then, he had run through some several simulations in neurospace before seeking and obtaining certification from Frank.

They talked mostly about these experiences—and what else he had been up to for the past three weeks—over the course of half an hour. Really, since his second day at the station, Anne and Jonah hadn't seen each other much at all.

Toward the end of their journey, the trees receded as the terrain climbed. A mountain rose up before them as Jonah progressively slowed the craft. Eventually they came to a stand still, hovering in the air above a peak among a series of peaks, before gently lowering.

"You might want this," Jonah said as he grabbed a nearby coat, "It can get a little chilly up here."

"Heh, where are we exactly?"

"Mount Haku."

"Mount Haku?" Anne asked with a twitch and a smile in surprise. "You sought out this mountain specifically for… some reason?"

"It's the first mountain I've ever known."

Anne breathed a quiet laugh of wonder, before following Jonah out of the craft into a breezy landscape of rock and dirt, intermingled with low-lying green scrub. After they both took a look around at the untouched scenery, Jonah retreated back into the craft and retrieved a massive backpack which he strapped over his puffy warm coat, along with a fairly formidable duffle bag he lugged around in his hand.

"Are you okay with a little hike?"

"Uh, sure. Did you need help with that?"

"No, no, I'm fine."

It wasn't a very long hike. Just long enough for Jonah to start to get winded. Anne followed along and shook her head with a smile behind Jonah's back, as he huffed and puffed his way up a steep incline. He insisted on carrying everything himself.

"H-here—*oof*—we are," Jonah said, struggling to catch his breath. He held out his arms wide, gesturing to their surroundings.

"And where's that?"

"The… *oof*… tallest… peak," Jonah explained. He set the bags down and caught his breath for a moment before continuing. "So… what do you think?"

"It's… beautiful," Anne remarked as she gazed off into rolling mists between distant peaks.

Jonah nodded. "I guess it's fitting then."

"Huh?"

Jonah replied by gesturing with open hands to Anne, inviting her to consider her own form.

"Oh!" Anne exclaimed before averting her eyes and laughing with a blush.

Jonah started unpacking, revealing a large checkered blanket which he promptly draped over the ground nearby. Next he pulled out several thermal bags, and set them down along with plates and other odds and ends.

"I thought this might be a lovely spot for a picnic."

Anne sniffed at the air. "Smells good. What did you get?"

"A number of things. One of them was, uh… kosher? Am I saying that right?"

"Huh?"

"It was spelled differently than I thought it would be, and I didn't seem to think 'kosher' was a single dish anyhow."

Confused, Anne stepped closer and peered down into the bag as Jonah held it open for her inspection. When she saw what it was, she started belting uproarious laughter. Jonah responded with confused chuckling. Anne started to blush again as she stopped and caught her breath.

"*Khuushuur.* You have khuushuur. How… how did you…?"

"How did I know?"

"Yeah."

"I bribed Julio."

"Really?"

"No," Jonah laughed. "He volunteered the data when I asked. He said he wasn't sure how it was pronounced, but said you ordered it at least once a week and seemed to really like it. Sorry for snooping. Just wanted it to be a surprise."

"That's okay. And… it is. Heh…"

Jonah took a piece, bit into it, chewed it over, and then exclaimed "This is really good! What is this exactly?"

"It's a kind of dumpling," Anne replied as she sat down and bit into one herself. "A century or two ago, they used to make it with animal flesh, back when that was common."

"Really?" Jonah replied, looking down at what he was eating.

"Yeah, but this is faux flesh, of course. It's usually mixed with spices and rolled into dough and fried."

"Hm."

"My great aunt Bayarmaa used to make this all the time," Anne noted wistfully.

"That's an interesting name…"

"It's Khangol."

"Khangol…" Jonah repeated and darted his eyes around.

"I'm guessing Ed hasn't taught you about that. It's a little obscure, heh."

"Just north of Zhuria among the eastern lands of Afar-Vesina."

"Impressive," Anne remarked genuinely.

"So is that where you're from then?"

"No, not really. My father was born there. And his father was from there, while his mother was from Zhuria. My own mother was of mostly Erilian descent."

"Oh, as in Erilinia off the coast of Vespour."

"Right, right. I'm pretty mixed I guess."

"Mixes are always the best. Just like this," Jonah said as he pointed at a dumpling in his hand before promptly taking a bite.

They sat and ate for the better part of an hour on the mountain top, admiring the natural beauty around them while enjoying each other's company. Anne herself was becoming keenly aware of how much she was enjoying the early evening, as the two shared a more intimate conversation than they ever had before.

He learned a number of things about Anne through the course of the conversation. Her father's name was Chinguun Ganbaatar. She inherited her father's given name as her surname, owing to Khangol tradition. Her mother, on the other hand, was a woman named Sophia McInnis, whose ancestry traced back to the northern reaches of Erilinia. Anne herself was born and raised in Maergland. Her father was a concert pianist, while her mother was a physicist. She followed in her mother's footsteps by becoming a biochemist.

"I'm sorry," Jonah stated at last, "Here I've been asking you about your past, your childhood, and things and…" He let out a sigh. "Well, I guess I wish I could… tell you about… well, you know."

"It's okay," Anne said. "It's kind of nice to be around someone who doesn't just talk about themselves all the time."

"Well, I think I've told you pretty much all there is to know at this point when it comes to *me*."

Anne gazed long into his gray eyes, before replying with a soft smile, "I'm not so sure that's true, Jonah."

"Heh," Jonah said, shifting his eyes with a touch of embarrassment.

Suddenly, her smile faded as she stared off into the distance with a sullen expression. "I just… I hope you can stay this way."

"What… what do you mean?" Jonah asked with concern.

"Jonah... I... I feel like I know who you are. Or at least know enough. I can see the kindness in your eyes. But... I don't really know who you *were*."

"Right. Me neither, heh."

She half smirked before continuing. "To be honest, I've lost people. People that were close to me. And that has kept me from getting close to others. I'm afraid to lose them. And there's a very real possibility that—"

"I... see," Jonah said with a sigh.

"I'm not sure that you do. I'm sorry before that I held things against you. Held it against you that you are—that you were... Kyrian."

"It's okay. From what I've heard, the Dominion is pretty —"

"It's not just the Dominion. It's Kyrianism as a whole... thing. I'm sure there's pockets of a more reasonable variety or something. At least that's what Ed keeps insisting. But my experience has been anything but."

"You don't have to talk about it if... if... you don't want."

"It's okay. I had a friend. A little over ten years ago. I was... seventeen at the time. His name was Josh. He was raised by Kyrian parents. I don't remember now what sect or whatever. But whatever it was, they were just..." She paused, let out a sigh, and shook her head. "Just... awful."

"Awful? How?"

"I mean, some parents can be relaxed and others pretty strict. They were definitely more on the strict side. A lot of seemingly strange and arbitrary rules. I didn't get it. And I didn't get how bad it could get until... until he came out."

"Came out?"

"It's an expression. In short, they found out about his boyfriend. He was gay."

"Oh…" Jonah stated with furrowed brow. "That's just like Julio, right? He's told me about his husband before."

"Heh… yeah. Except instead of being a lapsed Kosmic, my friend Josh was in a very strict fundamentalist home."

"Okay…" Jonah replied, still not understanding.

"Long story short, they kicked him out of the house and cut him off. They would have nothing to do with him. Kept him from seeing his sister and his brother."

Jonah gasped. "But why? What?"

"Heh, they called it 'tough love.'"

"What happened to him then? Was he okay?"

"My parents offered to help. Set him up on the couch in the den. It was fine for a couple days. But it wasn't enough help for him. He had all this… guilt… and pain. I guess he couldn't talk about it. And… I guess it was too much."

"I… what was—what do you mean?"

"He killed himself."

A sorrowful silence bore down between them. In that mournful moment, their eyes remained anchored to the ground in quiet reflection. Jonah was shocked, but somehow not surprised. The things he had heard from Ed. The stories he had been told. He didn't understand it all, but somehow he felt some acquaintance with the essence of its truth. Some feeling from the fog of his unremembered past seemed to confirm its veracity. And a strange mix of sadness and anger brought bitter tears to the edges of his eyes.

"Ed told me once something about the past. And the future, I guess. He said that 'time is an abstraction' and that all we really have is the present. It's the 'only time in which we live and only ever will.' I don't know about my past. And I certainly don't know what the future holds. But I know who I am right *now*, and how I feel about *you* right now. And... I don't know if that makes any sense."

"Hm, it does," Anne said with a smile. "Ed certainly has a share of wisdom."

Jonah nodded and gazed into her perfect emerald eyes.

Then with a wry smirk she continued, "But then sometimes he's so full of shit too."

They both laughed at her remark. Probably louder and longer than it deserved. But it helped to relieve the somber, mournful tension.

After a few minutes, they decided to head back to the craft. Anne insisted on helping this time, gathering up the duffle bag in her left hand as she walked along on his left. Seizing the opportunity, Jonah slowly extended out his left hand as they walked, and she returned the gesture with a smile as she placed her right hand in his. The delicate sensation sent tingles up his spine, and he breathed out a joyful sigh as they sauntered quietly back to the craft.

The flight back to the station was a pleasant one. And the conversation was as light as the craft. But it was grounded in something that was slowly growing between them. The words that weren't said were more meaningful than the ones which were. A lingering look. A knowing smile. This was the fertile soil they shared.

"I had a good time," Anne said when they reached her door.

"Me too," Jonah replied with a warm smirk and a long gaze. "I would love to do it again some time."

"Well, you know where to find me," Anne said playfully.

They laughed as they kept their eyes fixed on each other.

Jonah nodded with a wide grin. "I'll hunt you up soon then, if that's okay."

"Yeah. That sounds… good."

"Have a good night, Anne."

"You too, Jonah."

Jonah slowly sauntered back the short walk to his own little tree house with a perpetual smile on his face. The future was filled with excitement and wondrous possibility. It was a quiet, calm early evening. The stars just started to pop into a violet sky.

In the midst of that quiet, a strange sound suddenly presented itself to his ears. A kind of buzzing sound. A mosquito or a gnat. It was so oddly singular, so curiously out of place. He wouldn't have paid it a second thought, but he was suddenly reminded of that strange conversation Ed had with Anne days ago in neurospace. He wasn't sure what to make of that—if he was even entirely sure what it meant. But it filled his soul with a sense of foreboding.

He shrugged the ominous feeling away as he walked inside. It was too good of a night not to revel in its joy and hope.

ANOTHER day passed by, and then it was the start of the work week. Jonah was notably different when he came into Ed's office that day, and Ed wasn't sure whether to feel amused or annoyed. When he reflected on it, he figured it was probably a bit of both. Jonah was noticeably distracted. He still managed to be moderately productive, but with occasional sighs, quiet moans, and—perhaps most cringe-inducing—soft giggles.

"So..." Ed said and then coughed.

"Hmm?"

"I take it the date went well."

"What? Oh, uh, yeah yeah. I think she actually likes me."

"Well, I would figure as much considering she agreed to go out in the first place."

"Right, but I feel like there's a... like a... *connection* now."

Ed couldn't help but roll his eyes. For a moment, he almost regretted urging Jonah to ask out Anne. But then he quickly remembered it was good and right and perhaps... even fortuitous for everyone.

"I'm happy for you," Ed said. "For you both, that is. Just remember to tread lightly and slowly. There's plenty of time, and plenty of people. But I'm sure I'm beating a dead horse. We've talked about all that."

"Right, right. Idealization."

"Exactly."

A moment of silence passed while Jonah gazed off. With a furrowed brow, he slowly turned in his chair to face Ed. And Ed in turn turned toward Jonah.

"Hmm?" Ed asked.

"There was something else she mentioned. Something that... confused me... I guess."

"Oh, what's that?"

"Ed, why would someone's family... reject them... for loving someone?"

"Oh, wow... that's, uh..." Ed said with a deep sigh. "That's a tough question."

Jonah nodded soberly. Ed sighed again and gazed off for a moment, gathering his thoughts. Jonah waited patiently. He had become acquainted with Ed long enough to know when to let some silence sit in the room to give Ed a chance to articulate an answer to a tough question.

"The truth is, Jonah, there's never really a good reason. But there is an explanation. It all boils down to some measure of fear and disgust. Either or both, depending. It could take a number of different forms. The wrong religion. The wrong race. The wrong sex. The wrong tribal or political affiliation. In any of these cases, there's almost always some pressure to conform to some group dynamic. If someone is potentially looking to bind themselves to someone considered outside of some perceived group identity, then it threatens the stability or purity of the group. The latter is partly how disgust enters in. If the pairing is perceived to threaten the health and well-being of the group by introducing undesirable traits into the gene pool, for instance, this could be considered a threat to the group's future. It really depends on—"

"You mentioned the wrong sex?" Jonah interjected. "How does that play into what you're saying, exactly?"

"Ah, yes… That one is a pretty primitive taboo to be sure. I'm not an evolutionary biologist myself, but based on my own reading on the subject and private reasoning, it seems this has a lot to do with the historic evolution of the disgust response."

"What do you mean?"

"Well, how did you feel when you first learned Julio has a husband?"

"Confused, I guess. I didn't recall that being normal. Something almost felt… wrong, but I can't say why exactly. But then I got used to it, and that feeling kind of… faded away."

"Historically, a number of people have felt the same way," Ed said with a nod. "Unfortunately, they embraced that feeling rather than analyzing it. They built entire moral systems based on flawed precepts. It makes sense for most organisms to have some level of aversion to homosexual behavior. If our ancestors all practiced homosexual behavior exclusively, we wouldn't be here after all."

"Heh," Jonah chortled softly and nodded.

"The problem is that our personal tastes or distastes is not a sufficient basis for coherent and grounded moral reasoning. Even when that personal aesthetic may be shared by the majority of people. Aesthetic consensus is still aesthetic by nature. Beauty still remains in the eye of the beholder, even when we might all generally agree that symmetry is innately beautiful.

"We evolved symmetrically. It's a necessary aspect of cell division, after all. Asymmetrical morphology in an organism can often be an indicator of some genetic defect or chronic health condition impacting a potential parent's ability to produce healthy offspring or continue to care for that offspring.

"Of course, this only pertains to outward features. There is one notable asymmetrical feature of human beings that I personally find very beautiful." At that, Ed paused, prompting Jonah to ask the customary question.

"What's that?"

"The heart," Ed said with a smile. "It's placement in the chest cavity is off-center. It has to be on the right—from the perspective of someone facing the other, that is. And thus we say that a person has to have their heart 'in the right place.' When they do, it's a beautiful thing."

"Heh, okay."

"Well, to come full round to the point, there are a small minority of people who actually have their heart in the *left* place. It's a peculiar genetic condition called dextrocardia. It can either occur independently or as part of a condition of *situs inversus*. In the broader condition of situs inversus, a person's entire set of interior organs are reversed from their normal placement."

"Really?"

"Yes, indeed. We've known about it for centuries now. It doesn't usually impact day-to-day function or in any way requiring treatment, so it continues to be passed on and there remains a tiny minority of the populace who has these conditions."

"Huh… but what does that have to do with—with homosexuality, again?"

"Some people are born differently than the majority. The majority of people have some level of heterosexual impulse. But there are exceptions, and exceptions to the exceptions. Some people have an exclusively or majorly *homosexual* impulse. Some people have no sexual impulse at all. And others have some mixture of both. A tiny minority of individuals are born intersex, having ambiguous genitals or chromosomal makeup outside the sexual binary. And of course then there's the complexity of gender expression and dysphoria and how that plays into sexual attraction.

"The point is that human sexuality is complicated, but ultimately a matter of individual inclination and choice. There are some legitimate moral concerns related to sexuality, since it's an aspect of how we relate to one another. And how we should properly treat each other is the central question for any system of ethics.

"And on the individual level essentially boils down to 'Is anyone being hurt?'"

"Okay, so how are people getting hurt by... homosexual behavior?"

"Great question. Because the answer innately is *no one*. If it's sexual assault there's a clear victim, of course, but that would be just as true if it were heterosexual. The problem is that, for much of our history, people didn't necessarily formulate morality along purely these lines. Instead, they mixed it all up with aesthetics."

"What? Why?"

"Well, there's some valid reasons for that. We have a natural disgust response to corpses, for instance. And it was well and good that our ancestors had such a response. Touching a rotting corpse without taking adequate precautionary measures could be very deleterious to one's health and—by extension—the health of an entire community. It could introduce a person to all manner of potentially fatal pathogens. This is true of consuming feces or uncooked animal flesh—especially of the more carnivorous varieties higher up on the food chain.

"Of course, in the present day and age, we know how to take adequate precautions with scientifically validated best practices for hygiene and infection control. We could even bioengineer a simulated chunk of rotting wolf flesh, complete with crawling maggots, and yet make it perfectly safe for consumption.

"But thousands of years ago, ancient peoples didn't have these advantages. And so in those times certain people groups put taboos on consuming certain kinds of foods, interacting with corpses, and all manner of matters concerning public hygiene. This became intermingled with morality and—amongst those religious communities which continue to uphold ancient law codes—even theology."

"So… because ancient people were disgusted by homosexual behavior…" Jonah said and trailed off.

"It became a religiously ingrained taboo. And quite a strong one, especially amongst religious high control groups. As religious institutions faded away more than a century ago, we are mostly left with small pockets of high control groups. The one large exception, of course, being… the Kyrian Dominion."

"I see…"

"The ironic thing is that our present scientific progress in many ways started over a millennium ago, after some people decided to challenge taboos and handle corpses. It was through such clandestine investigations that we started to seriously learn about human anatomy and physiology."

"So… does the Dominion treat… gay people… like…"

"Not very well."

Jonah gulped, unsure if he wanted to know. He was afraid to know. But in the end he had to know. And so after a moment he finally asked. "What—what do they do?"

"They call it *reparative* therapy."

"What is that…?"

"Systematic torture. At least that's how I would describe it. Accounts vary, but essentially it's a pseudoscientific veneer covered over outdated and unethical behavioral conditioning, sometimes involving physical pain, mixed with a lot of guilt and fear induced either directly or left unaddressed by the broader culture of their society."

"Does it cause anyone to… to kill themselves?"

Ed nodded somberly. "I'm quite sure it does, yes. There's known cases, even if the Dominion seeks to hide it in assorted ways. Suicide is notably under-reported and hidden away when it occurs within Dominion borders. A source of shame amongst numerous others. Of course, a person could just choose to defect and leave the Dominion. They would be barred from re-entry and would be cut off from family and friends and possibly anyone they've ever known, but that is technically an option. Believe it or not, it's comparatively gentler than how Kyrian societies used to treat *sexual deviants* in times past."

"What do you mean?"

"It used to be a capital offense. Homosexuality amongst other things was punishable… by death."

Jonah's jaw went slack as he gazed off into space in horror and sorrow. Ed waited. He used the silence strategically. He wanted the point to sink in. He needed it to do so.

"T-thank you…" Jonah finally said before slowly turning back his chair. Ed simply nodded in return.

For the rest of the day, Jonah was mostly silent. He was very productive, losing himself in his work. Every so often he would gaze off in reflection and wipe away a quiet tear.

THE rest of that week, Jonah and Anne arranged to meet each other in the mess hall for lunch whenever they could, as well as meet at the same time for group exercise sessions coordinated in the evenings by Sumi. They managed to be relatively discrete—mostly thanks to Anne—but people still took notice of the two together. It was a small station and rumor spread quickly. But neither of them seemed to notice.

They mutually arranged to meet again for a night out at the end of the traditional work week. Her place. An hour "or so" after work. She messaged him on his terminal at home when she was done for the day, and then again approximately 70 minutes later as Jonah waited at home anxiously watching the onscreen clock.

He arrived at her door with a basket behind his back. When she answered, he almost felt like he was going to drop it. His jaw slowly descended involuntarily as he took in the sight of the woman who had answered the door.

Standing before him was a light golden goddess in a jet black dress. A form-fitting thin-strapped arm-less dress. And the form filling it was even more stunning. Deep amber hair delicately fluttering in the late twilight. Emerald eyes outlined with eyeliner and the softest hint of eye shadow. Amber red lipstick that complimented the long hair now framing her face.

"Hi there," she said with a smile.

"Wow…" he remarked in awe.

She laughed in turn and ever so slightly blushed.

"I mean, uh, yes, h-hi."

"I thought I'd dress a little more appropriately this time."

"Yeah…" he said, gawking. Then quickly collecting himself, he continued, "I mean, uh, you have a coat actually, right?"

"Oh, yes. Here…" she replied, grabbing a long black overcoat from a hook nearby. "I'm assuming we're going somewhere outdoors."

"Yes. Unless you'd prefer a candlelit dinner in the mess hall…"

They both laughed together as they headed out. He led her across the tree-lined walkways to the familiar platform which took them down to the ground below. From there he escorted her hand-in-hand to a craft as he had the week before.

"Where are we going this time?" she asked.

"It's a… *familiar*… surprise, this time."

She laughed when she saw where he had taken her. The lake shore. The very spot where they first met. It had been over a month and yet the stones were still there, encircling the scattered remains of the campfire he had started the night prior to their meeting.

"Seems so long ago. And yet just like yesterday," Jonah noted wistfully.

Anne simply nodded and observed him quietly. The failing light of the sun painted the stones with a hue of melancholic nostalgia. They may as well have been the ancient ruins of some long forgotten civilization. And that in turn reminded Jonah of Frank's report. Stonehenge site.

"So there's really other people here? Somewhere… on this planet?" he asked as he turned his eyes toward hers.

She nodded. "There *were*. Without a doubt. The evidence is overwhelming at this point. There's also a good amount of evidence that there still *are*. Humanoids very much like ourselves. I'm sure it's only a matter of time until we encounter one in the flesh."

Jonah lifted his eyes up to the trees surrounding the lake, glowing as they were in the crimson twilight, just as they did a month ago. It all seemed so familiar. Like a bygone conclusion of destiny that of course there should be such a place as this in the universe.

"Why does everything seem so *familiar* on this planet?" Jonah asked.

"Did Ed ever tell you why Talos Mystico was founded?"

"I think so. The day we met. He said the station was to study the flora and fauna originally."

"Right. More specifically, that's because the flora and fauna here—especially the flora—is remarkably solidial. The trees we're looking at are almost exactly like pine trees. Even down to their genome, they're incredibly similar."

So that explained it. Somehow the lack of strangeness made his surroundings seem all the more strange. Stranger still was his intrinsic familiarity with anything, considering he had no conscious recollection of Soyl. Indeed, he may never have lived there. It was as though the great world of his ancestral origin was embedded into his genes. Or perhaps some residue of it remained in his spirit. And then again, that may have simply been two different ways to say the same thing.

Then something flipped in his mind, and he saw the whole world upside down. What if this planet was his place of origin? And Soyl was simply somewhere else his race had migrated eons ago, before their space-faring technology was lost in the sands of time? Perhaps it started with a research station like Talos Mystico itself, abandoned in the midst of some interstellar conflict, in which they actually appeared to be. Could an entire civilization emerge on Solus 4 from the survivors? Perhaps two members of the station might have children, and those children might intermingle with the native inhabitants…

And then he gazed at Anne, as she gazed up at the darkening heavens. The two of them standing side by side on such strangely familiar ground, hand in hand. He was reminded of old myths and fables Ed had shared with him. Perhaps, to some future world, they would be Man and Woman. And this forest the very forest of Eternia. He looked across the water of the lake and imagined a fairy woman crossing it.

His feeling of whimsy turned to foreboding when he remembered those tales. For across the water, the she-fay brought the fall of Man and later the doom of Vaela. Whether he was to face his own failure or the dragon of transgression, either way was peril. As the land turned to night, a shadow covered his soul.

"Whether it's the Dominion or the Confederation, either way I'll be forced to remember…"

"What?"

"It's true, isn't it?"

"I… I don't know."

"Are you sure about that?"

"It's…" she began with a sigh. "It's probably… inevitable."

His eyes welled up with bitter tears. "I wish I could just stay here. I wish I could just hold on to this moment forever. I wish…"

She clasped his other hand as she stood in front of him, drawing attention to herself. "Take therefore no thought for the morrow: for the morrow shall take thought for the things of itself. Sufficient unto the day is the evil thereof."

He furrowed his brow and twitched his head. He almost recognized the quote. Finding it on her lips was surprising.

"Is that…?"

"From the Libben, yes. The words of the Meshek. Ed's right about one thing. There's wisdom everywhere… even in Kyrianism."

And with that they embraced. She rested her head on his shoulder and gently caressed his back with her warm comforting hands. He closed his eyes, rested his cheek against her soft luxuriant hair, and anointed her head with a single shed tear.

They let go of each other with a sigh and a smile. Looking gently down into her eyes, he gave a short embarrassed laugh. "So… are you hungry yet?"

"Heh…" she laughed with a warm smile and nodded. "Sure."

She helped him with the supplies he had brought to set out a large blanket, picnic basket, and a bottle of wine. He even had brought a little candelabra, which made her chortle when she saw it. In the still warm air of a quiet evening, they reclined across from one another, each propped up on an elbow as they ate seasoned clams, sipped at glasses of wine, and shared in frivolous flirtatious conversation.

They had finished their meal some time before they finished their frivolities. It was easier to sate their stomachs than to sate their souls. They may have stayed there some time longer, but for the wind. A cold breeze blew in, and they mutually decided to pack up and head back.

When they reached her door, hand in hand, at the end of their sauntering journey, she turned back to him mid-chortle. "So… would you… like to come inside?"

Jonah gave her the lecherous smirk of a teenage boy and a sudden wink. "Say again?"

She laughed and shook her head with an eye roll. "My apartment. Inside my apartment."

"I'd love to."

She led him inside and started to head toward the little kitchen alcove along the far wall. "I could pour you a cup of tea if you'd like."

He gently reached out and touched her side and ever so carefully pulled her back to him. "If it's all the same to you, I'd love to taste your lips instead…"

Her eyes widened and her cheeks flushed. Looking down with a quiet grin, she simply nodded her head. He leaned in and delicately pressed his lips against hers and kissed her gently. He slowly started to suck on her mouth as his arm reached around her back. He furtively parted her lips with his tongue, licking them inside and out. He tasted the roof of her mouth. The taste of wine. It went down sweetly. The sound of breathing grew louder in each other's ears as the wind from each other's noses blew on each other's cheeks. The smell of her nose was like apples.

Before long, they were clawing at each other's clothes. They were a whirlwind of passion, slowly storming itself to her chambers. They fell onto her green bed, the top sheet patterned as it was with lilies. He took a moment to stare into her green eyes against that green bed, as she pulled down her dress and exposed her heaving chest. The light in the room shined out from her eyes like two doves of light. Her breasts were like two fawns bounding over a hill as they moved with her heaving breaths.

He leaned in and kissed her neck. He kissed down her delicate long neck, his kisses descending a tower of ivory. She kissed his neck in turn. Desire overcame her. His sinewy flesh was strong and hard. He was like a cedar. As an apple tree among the trees of the wood. And she longed to taste his fruit. And so she playfully bit at his neck.

"Hmm?" he stopped, somewhat alarmed.

"I promise it won't hurt this time," she said playfully. They both laughed at the memory of when they met. And then he nodded and she continued. She sucked at his neck and occasionally bit it gently as she caressed his back.

"My turn," he whispered and kissed down her neck again, and then down her chest to her two beautiful breasts. There he suckled for a moment, enjoying the fruitage of her chest. A cluster of grapes. He enjoyed its sweetness, before continuing his descending kisses.

Her navel was as a round goblet. He licked inside it, tasting the dew of her sweat. She laughed at the tickling sensation, and he continued.

He removed her dress completely and caressed her legs. The joints of her thighs were like jewels, the work of the hands of a cunning workman. And tracing down between her milky thighs was a garden. In the middle of her garden lay a door. Behind that door lay a deeper navel. A round goblet whose liquor was no mere sweat. And at this point her cup was overflowing. He put his hand by the hole of the door, and her bowels were moved for him. He returned to her breasts as he kept his hand at her door.

He kissed her with the kisses of his mouth. His love was better than wine. An aroma wafted between them. The natural perfume of her body was a pleasant fragrance in his nose. And she indulged in his scent as well. His head was as a sachet of myrh between her breasts.

She opened herself to him with her fingers. Her hands became drenched in fluid myrh, her fingers dripped with sweet smelling myrh. And so he went down to her garden to see the fruitage of her valley. He parted her lips and enjoyed the flourishing vine of her vineyard. The sweet-tart pomegranate within.

The spiced wine of her pomegranate was overflowing, and she could hardly stand it any longer. She pushed with her fingers on his triceps, signaling him to arise. His marble legs came between her own. She caressed the rippling muscles of his bare chest. Panting like a gazelle in flight, she urged him to enter.

And so he entered her garden at last. The snake had made its way through the underbrush to the trunk of her tree. The tree of life she held inside, with its branches to either side.

And thus did he know her. And he took pleasure in that knowledge. And she took pleasure in his taking. And her taking gave him pleasure to take. And thus giving and taking coiled around between and within them.

Long had this knowledge come to be associated with transgression. And a part of him felt that. It was the loss of innocence that came with knowledge. A necessary loss, just as death was necessary for life. Thus, it brought forth both death and life, and his eyes were opened. Two dilated pupils gazing at her form in awe.

But the real transgression would be imbalance. For in truth that feeling he had—the reveling in transgression, the delight in getting away with something like a child with his hand in the cookie jar—was itself a necessary impulse. For to obey the first command—to multiply, subdue, and have dominion—was quite literally against nature. And yet it was nature that had produced this impulse. Thus, to obey this command was to transgress against the very source of the commandment. Yet, like the mother of Oedipus, the Great Mother became the bride of Man and cried "take me" to the son she had produced.

But this was no tragedy. Consciousness precipitated a paradox, and its resolution lay in balance. The harmony lay in taking only that which was given and giving only what would be taken. In this manner the impulse—to take, subdue, and bend the world to one's will—could be indulged with impunity.

And so he did indulge. They indulged in each other. Giving love and taking love—making love throughout the night. They went to sleep in each other's arms, and thus ended the first of many evenings they would share together.

FOUR months passed. Only a few weeks before the next transport from the Confederation was scheduled to arrive and the current crew—Jonah included—was to be rotated out. In the meantime, Jonah became increasingly embedded in the little society of Talos Mystico. He made it a routine to join in group exercise sessions in the early evenings, and played cards and board games with Frank and Sumi on weekends. He continued to meet with Ed nearly every day, but he also went out and about to assist everyone in the station with all manner of technological odds and ends. Helping Dr. Jenkins archive her correspondences one day. Assisting Frank with mapping topology data in neurospace, another.

Jonah's ancient library simulation in neurospace actually became something of a popular hub. Half a dozen scientists were milling around the space one day, while Jonah was configuring settings on a floating panel along one of the walls of the great hall.

"Hey there," Anne said as she tapped Jonah on the shoulder.

"Oh hey!" Jonah said with a wide grin as he turned around to face her.

"You coming home any time soon, stranger?"

"Oh yeah, sorry, I just had some quick updates I wanted to make. I'm just about done now."

"No rush. I just got in from the lab right before I dropped in. I'll probably have an hour or two. Just thought it'd be nice to have you around."

"You could work in here if you want."

"It's just not the same. Besides…" She leaned in, embraced him, and whispered in his ear, "…prying eyes and all that."

He looked around and noticed a couple of folks sitting along the far wall staring back at him, before quickly averting their eyes. "Heh, okay. I'll leave in a minute…"

"I love you," she whispered.

"I love you too," he whispered back and kissed her cheek.

"Oh, do you think you could pick up some fresh cabbage from the vivarium on your way back?"

"Sure thing."

"I have a new recipe I wanna try out."

"I thought I was cooking tonight."

"Yeah, for tomorrow night. Just want to make sure I have some first."

"Okay, I'll requisition a head before Sumi steals them all."

"Heh, good idea. See you soon then."

"See you soon."

After a quick kiss goodbye, she disappeared, and Jonah returned to his work. A few moments later he was done, and so he exited. He would have said goodbye to Ed, but he was still jacked in, lying on the other side of the room motionless apart from the occasional subtle heaving motions of his torso from the massaging rollers beneath him.

Jonah collected his coat and headed out into the cold crisp air outside. He quickly jogged over to his old apartment. He figured while he was at the vivarium he could pick a few rose stems. It was Anne's birthday in two days. He would stash the flowers away along with a gift he had hidden.

The door slid open to an apartment as lonely and barren as the day he first entered it. He turned on the light and headed to the material modeler in the kitchen. There he tapped away on its controls, and selected the glass model he picked out in neuro earlier. In less than a minute, he had a perfectly lovely little vase. In the meantime, he sauntered over to the little chest of drawers next to his old bed.

He pulled out the bottom drawer and looked at the little object inside. A bowl, crumpled up in gift wrap. It was a traditional Khangol copper bowl, ornately engraved and inlaid with mahogany wood. He had spent the better part of a week through a series of trades to procure the raw materials for the vessel. The unmanned supply ship only arrived a day ago, and he rushed to have it replicated from the blueprint he had on file. The final product took an hour, and three different manufacturing runs to fabricate.

Upon closing the shelf with a smile, he heard a tinkling jangling sound. With narrowed eyes, he opened the top shelf and discovered his old golden necklace. The peculiar amulet, laying neglected. He had forgotten he left it there.

After filling up the vase with water, he set it on a counter and rushed out the door. He made his way down to the snowy surface of the forest floor and across the powdery clearing to the vivarium in the chilly late afternoon of what could be called a winter's day on Solus 4. As he walked across the open field, something in his peripheral vision momentarily caught his attention. The shadow of some figure out in the woods.

He stopped and looked long into and between the trees, waiting to see if he noticed it again.

Some kind of motion. And the faint crunchy sound of rustling steps amidst the underbrush and snow in the distance. Jonah cautiously stepped toward the tree line, gripping his plasma pistol. There was an occasion once or twice within the past few months when large beasts had been spotted crossing near the tree line. It would be good to know if that was the case, so it might not catch anyone else at unawares.

Jonah slowly sauntered past the tree line into the forest, pistol in hand. After a few soft crunchy paces in, he stopped and looked around, seeing if he could spot any motion again. Whatever it was seemed to have stopped. It likely noted his presence and was waiting him out.

He took a moment to admire the golden sunlight streaming through the white-topped canopy overhead. Watched the fog of his breath float through the air. Then the sound came again. And the form in the distance. He could have sworn it was humanoid.

His heart raced a little. Could this be first contact? An actual glimpse of the native inhabitants? He was probably getting ahead of himself. His friends had been scouring the planet for close to a year. One of them just happening to show up on his doorstep while he had the honor of being the first seemed like some kind of absurdly hopeful hubris. But then, it moved again, and the distant figure definitely moved just like a man.

In the next moment, another thought occurred to him, and his heart raced even more. He tightened his pistol and gulped. Perhaps that figure *was* humanoid, and actually human specifically. And if so, that could mean…

"Move! Move!" the figure shouted and rushed toward him.

He instinctively turned and ran, but he didn't get very far. A low murmur rumbled all around him, and he almost instantly felt his muscles seize. Tinnitus ringed in his ears as he fell forward into the snow. As the world faded to black, he struggled to whisper a single word: "Anne…"

DARKNESS. It's not nothing. If it were, it couldn't be seen. It would be like the visual experience of what lies beyond one's peripheral vision. That is to say, no experience at all. The human mind is actually quite comfortable with the void. It encounters it routinely. Whether it's the sight that cannot be seen or the sound of the proverbial tree in the forest. That which lies beyond the realm of experience is simply ignored or re-imagined, like the little lies one's eyes tell in the midst of their blind spots.

It is not venturing into the void that chills the heart of men. On the contrary, this brings excitement and the greatest of joys. It is the heart of adventure. When the unknown can be faced and conquered—a light shone into the dark—the heart is stilled, and filled with peace.

What makes men shudder is not the void, but the dark. The experience of seeing when there is nothing to be seen—but seeing nevertheless. It is the terrible awareness of space filled with the unknown. A dark abyss like an inky sea, and who knows what lies in the deep? It could be potentially populated with the most horrible of conceivable horrors, or—worse yet—terrors that lie beyond even the imagination.

Most men will not face the darkest dark. Even on a moonless night, the stars remain. Even in the deep black of a light-less cave, the eyes still produce the phantom photopsias of eigengrau. And in the soundless silence of the most empty of aural privation there remains the little murmurs of organs, the sonorous breeze of breath, and any number of countless sounds that normally go unnoticed.

But no such mercy was afforded to Jonah. He found himself in the blackest of blacks. The awareness of a space seen without eyes, whose dimensions were unfathomably vast and may as well have been infinite. The completely still quiet of absolute deafness. Not even the reassuring sensation of a body, except in the vaguest of ways, like the sensation of a phantom limb—except it was his entire body which had been amputated. He was as a disembodied spirit floating in the depths of a living hell. Which is of course the only kind of hell which can be experienced, as experience and life go hand in hand.

And Jonah was indeed alive. Although for some agonizing untold amount of time he wondered in terror if he were not. Terror gave way to despair. A sinking feeling in a phantom gut. The vague sensation of a sad face he couldn't see. But then one could never see one's face as others might see it. Even the most reflective of surfaces absorb some of the light which reflects. And when it does, the image is reversed. It's the visual equivalent to the sound of one's own voice in a recording—an even greater sensory disparity in one's sense of self.

If he had a face, at least he could cry. He would weep wet tears down his cheeks as he wailed with his mouth. That, at least, would be some sort of release. He tried imagining screaming, and he could almost feel it. The phantom feeling teased his soul with its intangible tangibility. There would be no release, only the sinking feeling of despair and a growing melancholy.

His unbounded sadness and self-pity suddenly turned to anger. Unbounded wrath welled up inside his shadowy soul. If he was to be kept in such a cage of darkness, he would not go gently into that good night. He would "rage against the dying of the light."[2] Words he recalled from he knew not where.

But there was nowhere to direct his rage. The fire of his wrath would produce no light. There were no bars to bite. And no teeth with which to bite them. And so he quickly fell into despair.

Ed had once told him, "Apart from loss, what we really fear in death is not death itself but the gloomy thought of being bound up forever and ever in the dark. If it is true that we cease to exist upon death—who can say for sure?—then death is not something to be experienced. Dying, perhaps, but not death itself. It is as though the entire world doesn't exist and never has. Death would be precisely the same kind of experience as we had before our earliest memory. An unfathomable void beyond experience. So instead, when we recoil at the thought of death, when we really think it through, this is really a fear of being *trapped*. And our animal instincts cannot stand for that. We recoil at being stuck in a cage and so naturally we react. Our heart races and we immediately seek escape."

He had delivered this diatribe amidst a much longer rant. In bitterness, Jonah recalled it. It seemed like Ed was wrong and Anne was right. What was it she said about him? "Full of shit." If he had teeth, Jonah would have ground them.

At that very moment, though, something strange happened. Entering into his phantom awareness was the very sound of Ed's voice. As he was recalling what Ed had said, he was actually *hearing* his voice—or perhaps imagining the sound. But then, what was really the difference? If he imagined that sound strongly enough, could he hear it more clearly? Perhaps he didn't need ears after all. Or perhaps he could imagine them well enough. Perhaps he could imagine the entire universe back into existence—or maybe an entirely new one. Perhaps he had only to say to himself "Let there be light" and he would have it. His own world, fashioned according to his imagination.

The thought excited hope in his desperate phantom heart. He could get through this. He could transmute it. He had faced darkness before. Twinkling lights in the dark. As he thought of them, they appeared. Along with the faint red flash revealing rolling clouds of smoke. And he heard the buzz saw sound of the alarm. He could even almost detect the sharp smell of burning plastic.

Jonah hovered over the waters of a new world. It wasn't completely in focus, but there were tantalizing glimpses. Sights and sounds started to swirl round in the space all around him. It might take hours or days, but given enough time, who knew what might be possible?

He felt as though he were starting to go mad. But in a world with all the madness he could recall, perhaps it only made sense that it would be the product of a madman. Perhaps he was that madman all along and the darkness was simply a return to his natural state. An intolerable state from which he would retreat and create the world again. The madness of maya emerging to alleviate his silent suffering.

After this went on for some time—how long he could never be sure—the sights and sounds grew ever more vivid, and then his own sense of self started to dissolve. It was as though he merged with the world he was making, experiencer becoming experience. Pure experience. Sights without seeing. Sensations without sensing. Random bits of thoughts without a thinker. He was lost in the deep, floating away with the tide.

He would later recall that it was actually becoming quite a pleasant experience. But for now there was no one to please, and that made the pleasure all the more pure.

It eventually ended. A little light at the center of his vision suddenly expanded. It was accompanied by growing sound. His entire field of view was filled with something. It was dark. But it was a natural dark. A real dark. Rather than the pure black of pure imagination, he was instead confronted with… something. A room? It looked like there were twinkling lights in the distance. What were they? Stars.

The realization shook him into self-awareness, as did the tingling sensations all over his body. A very real body that he was quickly starting to feel. It was exactly like the sensation of returning from neurospace. Neurospace? Is that where he had been?

"You dropped him into limbo?" a man asked with more than a hint of anger.

"Relax, he's okay. It was only an hour and a half," someone else with a low gruff voice replied.

An hour or so? Was that all it was? It seemed like a lot longer. Although when he thought about it, it also somehow seemed shorter. Time was distorted in that space.

"Chris! Are you okay, Chris? It's me, Josh. You're back, my friend!"

That was the first man. Who were these people? He waited to hear Chris's response, but it never came. He slowly shifted his eyes around the room. Where was he? A rectangular field of stars, like through a window. Vague bits of gray in a dark room. Everything was dark. Two shadows loomed over him. As his vision became clearer, he saw they were faces. Two strange men were standing next to him, towering above him in the gloom, while he remained reclined.

"The One help you if he's hurt!" shouted one man to the other. It was the man who called himself Josh.

"I'm telling you, he's perfectly fine. I know a guy who drops into limbo for fun. Says it's relaxing."

"I'm sure this *guy* has never been *thrown* into it by a squad of goons."

"Did you seriously just call Alpha team a 'squad of goons?'"

"If the boot fits. Your people lack subtlety and finesse."

"We're not content to sit in the shadows and do nothing like you Kalevites."

"You should be careful around people who sit in shadows. In the cover of dark, you'll never see the blade coming for your back."

"Why you son of a—"

"Gentlemen!" a third voice called out from the dark. The gravelly voice of an older man. "The body has different members with different gifts. It does no good to quarrel."

"Yes, Rector," Josh replied with a conceding tone and bowed his head. The other man with the gruff voice simply nodded with a grunt.

"Now then, I'm sure we're all more than grateful to have our dear Brother Tyler back with us," the older man said dryly in a cold monotone. "But there remains the matter of this procedure. Our brother is in need of healing and restoration."

Tyler. The word sent shivers down Jonah's spine and sent his heart racing. They were talking about him. And the word *restoration* carried with it ominous overtones.

Jonah jerked at his limbs as to flee. But that's when he felt the restraints. They wrapped around his ankles and wrists. He was helplessly immobile there in the dark. Up until now he had listened quietly, stilling his voice out of caution. But now that he understood the nature of his predicament, he might as well clamor.

"Let me out! You can't do this! No!"

"It's okay, Chris! You're safe now!" Josh exclaimed.

"No! Stop! I don't consent to this! Please let me out!"

"*Consent…?*" Josh replied with genuine confusion.

"Heh," the gruff man said, "you see why we had to drop him now? He was waving around a pistol when we found him."

"It would be better for our dear brother if we start sooner than later," the older man coolly observed.

Jonah's mind raced. He frantically analyzed the situation and tried to recall anything that might help. An old conversation with Ed came to him. Words popped into his head and he quickly uttered them. "Elventia accords! P-per the Elventia Accords, I cannot be made to undergo any medical procedures without—without my consent."

His statement was met with silence and awkward shuffling. All those weeks listening to Ed talk about law and politics—amongst myriad other subjects. They may have actually proved useful now. Perhaps these may have been the magic words that would save him. His heart raced while he waited for a reply with eager hope.

"W-what is he talking about…?" Josh asked toward the older man.

A low menacing chuckle rolled out from the dark. It made Jonah's blood run cold. It was the older man. Once he was done with his rumbling laugh, he said, "Elventia Accords. Consent. Soon our dear confused brother will start talking about the consent of the governed, religious liberty, and other such secular nonsense. They really tried their best to brainwash you, didn't they, Brother Tyler?"

"Why are you doing this to me? I don't want it. It's not right!"

The older man ignored Jonah's clamor and continued lecturing like an old schoolmaster, "You see, Brother Tyler, we do not recognize the validity of arbitrary law. Our law is The

One's law, and we must obey The One rather than men. Your thinking needs to be adjusted."

"The system should be ready now, Rector Falwell," a fourth man said from some unseen corner of the room.

"Very good. Let us not dally any longer, gentlemen."

Long even breaths. He had to calm the storm of his panic. Jonah shifted into a state of hyper-awareness as he sought out options. Negotiation and reasoning would be fruitless. He had to resist these restraints. He gently tugged at them with his ankles. Thick cold metal. No budging. Perhaps if he could find something to pick them. A thin wire of some sort. Where could he get possibly get one?

His mind raced to other options. Perhaps he could try words again somehow. The one man nearby. The one calling himself Josh. He seemed the most sympathetic. His words and their tone conveyed some kind of genuine friendship.

"Sorry, sir, it may be a couple minutes before we can get a decryption lock on the device," the man in the distance explained. "The onboard nanoclock has become out of sync. It will take a little time to make the needed adjustments. This is the first time we've had a veil running longer than a week."

"Understood," the gravel-voiced rector replied. "These are indeed extraordinary circumstances. Please take as much time as needed… but no longer."

Now was Jonah's chance. His only chance. He turned to the young man hovering over him in the gloom. The only one that might present an opportunity.

"Josh…" Jonah uttered quietly.

"Yes, Chris?" Josh asked as he placed his hand on Jonah's shoulder and leaned in closer.

Why did he keep calling him that name? A mystery for another day. Jonah shrugged it off and replied in a near-whisper, "Josh, you can't let them do this to me…"

"It's going to be okay, my friend. You've been out of it for so long. I know it's confusing."

"I… I don't want to remember. And I don't want to forget."

"What do you mean? What is it you don't want to remember? Or—or forget?"

"I like who I am now. I've gained so much. Ed and Anne. I have a whole life now. Ed has told me so much about—about all this."

Jonah's last sentence was a misstep. He could feel it when Josh pulled back. His tone changed slightly as Josh interjected, "Lies. You've been fed a lot of lies, my friend. That station where you were. Those people. They don't understand. They probably never will. They're outsiders."

"O-okay, okay… but… I just need some time. Can you please just tell them to stop? For now. That's all. I just need… some time."

"I… I don't think that… that that's…"

"We're ready to begin now, sir," the man in the distance said as he tapped away on something in the dark.

"Excellent," the old rector rumbled. "Proceed."

With a whir, Jonah felt the kind of stretcher upon which he was lying start to lower. His head was positioned between something. He could detect the subtle change in ambient sound. Something was next to each ear on either side of his head.

"No, Josh, please. Don't let them do this!"

Josh pulled away and shook his head.

Jonah understood now entirely how Anne must have felt the day they met. He regretted more than ever having scared her so. The fear he had for his life was paralyzing—not that there was anywhere to move at this point. He understood too the longing to grasp at straws and call out into the universe to anything or anyone that might in the remotest possibility bring some kind of deliverance.

"Oh dear god…" he uttered as he closed his eyes in despair.

"Hmph, see how he mutters like a pagan," the old rector stated with disgust. "So sad."

"Unto the heathen there are many gods and lords," Josh recited from the dark. "But for us, there are no gods. There is only The One."

"Well said, Brother Branch. Well said."

A low hum started to murmur in Jonah's ears as something like a visor rolled over his face, blocking out his vision. His head was entirely encased now, as the low hum continued in his ears. This was it. This was the end. He was utterly alone. Alone in the dark.

But he had faced the dark before. He came through it. He could come through this too. In the end, taking responsibility and trusting in himself was more empowering and comforting than reaching out for any crutch outside. He made peace with the loss. It too was something he had encountered before.

"Heh," Jonah laughed sardonically with a tear in his eye. "I never got her the cabbage…"

HE found himself on the front porch of an old house. He had no idea how long he had been standing there. It might as well have been forever. White wood railings to match the white wood panels of the house. It was as quaint as it was antiquated. He had the vague awareness of two stories below a pitched roof, but he never actually saw it.

He turned the handle on the front door and slowly opened it. It made a long creaking sound as he delicately pushed it open on its old hinges. Inside, the house looked somewhat neglected, but not terribly so. It looked recently vacated, perhaps a few weeks or months. A long vacation, perhaps. But all the furniture was there. Some of them covered in white sheets for some reason, but there, nevertheless. An old grandfather clock ticked away along the far wall as he entered.

Dust bunnies and smaller particles swirled in the air, most visible in the golden light streaming through the windows. The air was a little stuffy but not suffocating. The interior was dim, with everything cast in a golden brown hue.

He felt drawn inside, but not pulled against his will. It all seemed perfectly natural, like responding to some homing instinct. Every step forward was one he chose, and yet was also somehow chosen for him. It was like home, yet strange at the same time.

That same force, that same instinct, which drew him forward led him to an open door. An entryway to a flight of stairs leading down into darkness. It made him uneasy to proceed, but felt he must. And so he stepped down and down, further into the dark. The stairs led to a wall and then turned sharply to another flight of steps. A dim light came from his right, and as he turned to the second set of steps down, he saw the stairs were leading him into an opening. An open space of some large basement appeared before him.

At the very bottom, the basement floor was dirt. And as he stepped onto that dirt, he became aware of a great cacophony. A great mess of sound from dozens of voices in that dim, dusty space. Along all the walls was a crowd of people. Many of them were watching him carefully. Some of them were ambivalent. Most of them started cheering and shouting at his arrival. But it wasn't so much that they were cheering for him out of personal support. It was more like the cheers of a drunken mob excited to see some makeshift bomb explode. It made him very uneasy, but he felt he had to keep going nevertheless.

In the center of that open space, taking up most of the room, was a great circular cage. It was a crude cage made of old chain link fencing. On one side of the cage facing him was an opening. A kind of door made out of the same fencing material that for the time stood open.

He walked through the door, floating along on his feet as though carried by the current of some stream. The door was closed behind him. And locked. This gave him no cause for alarm. He didn't even acknowledge it. This was his place. He didn't enjoy where he was, but it was his place nevertheless. The dust in the air. The smell of sweat and grease. The dark wet spots on the ground here and there that looked like oil, but somehow he knew was blood.

"Ladies and gentlemen!" a voice boomed out from some staticky loudspeaker.

"Who ya talkin' to? I don't see nobody like that 'ere!" shouted a big, bald, fat man in the crowd before taking a swig out of a bottle in his hand. The crowd erupted into laughter. Somehow sinister laughter.

The voice continued, making no acknowledgment of the remark, "You know our contestants. And they've known each other from afar for some time. But their feud is just beginning. So without further ado…"

In the middle of the voice's dramatic pause, someone else in the crowd stepped forward and stood on their tiptoes, extended a limp wrist, and bobbled their head as they called out "Adieu!" with a mockingly exaggerated accent. The crowd erupted into laughter once more before the voice continued, "Let's see some blood!"

A bell rang out, and the crowd roared. He knew that was his signal to fight. He stepped forward to face his opponent on the opposite side of the crude ring. Staring back at him with a monstrously mean expression… was his own face.

And that's when his perspective shifted. And he was that man. And the man he was before was looking back at himself with a somber, but determined face. He despised that man. The man who had made his way down into the basement late. The man who dared threaten to usurp him. The young upstart who had the monumental audacity to challenge his throne.

And his perspective shifted back again. He loathed the man across from him. The man who had spent so long in the dark collecting dust and grime, spending most of his time cleaning the house's white exterior while neglecting its interior —especially the basement. Dirt and grime and malice hidden away in the dark. It could have been a true home fit for a king, but he had let its foundation rot. And now it was little more than a whitewashed tomb.

And so he circled himself. The two exchanged blows. Two topless, barefoot warriors with tattered rags for shorts. They battered each other mercilessly. Bruising each other's sinewy flesh with their fists and feet. Breaking the skin open with their blows to pour blood on the dust.

They both paused for a moment to catch their breath. That was when he caught sight of something. The latecomer caught sight of it. Caught sight of him. Another someone. A boy curled up in a ball against the far cage wall. Alone and afraid.

"Who is that?" he asked himself.

"Leave him out of this!" the other older him growled.

And so he came at himself. And the two fought once more. But the latecomer watched the boy intently as they fought. He winced at every blow. Any time either were hit, he winced. It was as though the boy could feel every scrape and bruise. The boy was himself battered, and his pain was being multiplied as they fought. Thus he remained curled up, crying in the corner.

And his perspective shifted once more, but this time it was different. He was still the latecomer, but behind the old king's eyes, as though he had simply left his body. But he could also feel the old king's feelings. He understood now. He was protecting the boy, keeping him down in the dim dusty basement away from the threats of the world outside.

When he returned to himself, the latecomer dropped his fists and let them unfurl. He knew what he had to do, no matter the cost. While he had recognized his own *face* in the man's, it was only now that he had come to recognize *himself.*

"Do what you must," the latecomer said to the king. He extended his palms out to his sides in a gesture of peace. He relaxed the muscles of his face and closed his eyes.

"I will!" the wrathful king shouted as he grabbed a giant rusty nail nearby. Without a moment's hesitation, he thrust the nail into the other's chest deeply and firmly. Blood poured forth like a fountain from the latecomer's chest. It exploded in fact, covering he, himself, and the boy in the blood from head to toe. A dragon's roar was heard, and the entire room filled with flames.

The blood of the beast had spared his life from the flames. The words whispered in his ears. Which set he didn't know. It didn't matter anymore. He was both Vaela and Har-martia. The dragon slayer and the dragon. The great serpent who must be lifted up. Just as with any man who had finally found true peace with himself.

Trap doors in the four walls of the basement opened and revealed different color gems in each. Light shone from the gems, intersecting at the point of the two combatants in the center. The latecomer embraced the old king as the entire basement filled with a bright light. Everything became brilliant shining white, before fading back to an undifferentiated darkness. The darkness he saw as he slowly opened his eyes and awakened from the dream.

WHEN he awoke, it was with a kind of double-vision. To say he was disoriented would be an understatement. He wasn't entirely sure where he was. But more pertinently, he wasn't sure *who* he was. When he silently asked himself, he got back two replies. *Jonah. Chris.*

But of course, he knew both answers were technically correct. His full name after all was Jonah Christoff Tyler. *So that was what the C stood for.* That was the Jonah in him. The Chris in him could only roll his eyes at such irritating ignorance.

His experience was like the silhouette of the spinning dancer. An optical illusion where—to start—the dancer spins clockwise. Watched for a while, and it may spin the other way, counter-clockwise. Watched even longer—and perhaps with some effort—the dancer "spins" both ways simultaneously, like a jumble of wobbly limbs jostling left and right.

In the confusion of waking, he tried to recall what happened the day prior. Seen one way, yesterday was the dark room with the window out to stars, filled with frightful figures and the looming threat of a kind of death. Seen another way, "yesterday" ended in the engineering section of the vessel he had boarded just a few days prior—the MS Pescha—when a sudden explosion rocked the engine compartment and chaos erupted. The dancer spun and spun, and he could see it either way.

Seen one way, he had been asleep for a long time with a dream filled with dreams within the dream, but the weight of its vividness and sense of time could not be ignored. Seen another way, his life only began a few months ago and everything prior was a set of experiences he was only now inheriting. But the inheritance was too large and overwhelming for him to claim as his own, yet he knew that's precisely what it was. And thus the dancer spun both ways, and he could see the fundamental unity underlying his experiences. The unity of persons within himself.

"Chris…? Are you awake?"

It was a voice he recognized. A voice from the dream and a voice from before it. Or a voice from the day before and a voice from the tidal wave of experiences crashing down over him. Either way, he recognized this man. His old friend Joshua Branch.

"Josh…" he said groggily. Even as he said the name, he felt a strange shudder of recognition. Strange, as he recognized the name in two very different ways.

"Do you mind if I turn on the light?"

"Go ahead."

Josh was careful to slowly turn up the light in the room, adjusting the knob smoothly to make the light grow like a gradual sunrise. He left it at as a dim orange glow and came back to his bed side.

Tyler took in his surroundings. It was a sparse interior. If it weren't for the warm orange glow, the walls would be white. It was a cozy small room. No windows. A simple sliding door to his right, with his bed to the left. On the far wall ahead, he could see the room's sole decoration. A wooden "eye." At least that's what it was called. It was a very abstract symbol. A perfect circle bisected by a line segment.

Seeing it, he was reminded of his old necklace. He grasped at his chest to find it bare. That's when he remembered it wasn't there anymore. He had left it back in his treehouse apartment, stored away in a little shelf. Its absence was a tangible reminder of the reality of those months.

"Are we on the Selenium?" Tyler croaked as he rubbed his eyes.

"Yes, indeed… It's good to have you back, Chris."

Tyler slowly nodded and ran his fingers through his hair. "How long have I been out?"

"Around twelve hours now."

Tyler's eyes grew wide. "Really…?"

Josh quietly nodded and smiled. "Healing Hands gave Command a notice of orders on your behalf for a suspension of duty for seven days."

Tyler nodded. "I feel like I'm gonna need it."

"I'm sure you'll be feeling like yourself in no time."

Tyler furrowed his brow. "What do you mean…?"

"Just, you know… feeling better."

"Right… right…"

"Hey, maybe we can dive into neuro together later. There's a new shooting sim Jake introduced me to."

"Maybe later…"

"Yeah, of course. Just whenever."

Tyler closed his eyes for a bit while Josh waited nearby patiently. He finally spoke up in a croaking voice, his eyes still closed. "I think I want to be alone for a while."

"Sure, sure. I'll get out of your hair. I'm sure it's been a while since you got back to your private sim collection, eh?" Josh asked with a snicker.

Tyler quickly grew irritated at the suggestion of what Josh was implying. "Please go" he stated with a clenched jaw, trying to still be polite but failing slightly with his tone. He felt more than justified nevertheless.

"Okay… yeah, sure…" Josh said, slightly hurt and a little confused at Tyler's tone. He slowly rose up and walked out without another word.

Tyler breathed a sigh of relief as his old friend left. He had a lot to think about.

He spent an hour or two reflecting on the past. His past. His childhood on Helios 3. His parent's divorce and his subsequent move to Kolob 6. He told himself the story of his life from the beginning as he paced his dim little room. The room he had called home for the better part of a year after he had transferred to serve onboard the Selenium.

He had been between tours of duty when he was returning to the ship. He had a routine stop at Furca Major—a spaceport orbiting Darmaseq 4. At that point, there were two vessels scheduled to rendezvous with the Selenium. The Pescha and the Artos. The Artos was actually scheduled to depart sooner by a couple of hours, but a poster for a new production showing at the station's holocinema attracted his attention. He decided to grab a bite to eat and give it a look. And so he decided to wait for the Pescha.

He wondered at the thought of how fateful that decision had been. But then wasn't every decision really like that? Every choice. Every fork in the road. Like little stones in a pool, they smash into the watery surface of the world and send out ripples far beyond the initial time and place of their impact. And those ripples hit other ripples, creating interface patterns. Some amplify the waves, while others cancel them out. And these stones are cast out onto the water moment after moment, creating incalculable complexity.

Reformists tended to split over the issue—like most every other issue—while Kosmics and the Kyrios of the East embraced it as a mystery. The words came to him with a specific voice. Whose voice was that? Ed's voice. A quote from the past. A voice from the dream, which was quickly growing real. A part of him scoffed at such commentary as a matter of course. A knee-jerk reaction to the mere presence of such a voice in his soul. But another part, a deeper part, had to admit to its truth. It wasn't even controversial. The Reformist tradition—his own tradition, effectively—had been steeped in debates about the nature of choice. The One's and Man's. At stake was the sovereignty of one and the liberty of the other.

Obviously liberty was relative, he told himself. Sovereignty could trump it while still keeping a measure of liberty intact. Why would it need to be absolute?

But a more interesting thought to me is... what would things be like from The One's perspective? If The One can long for anything—and he must if he can truly be called "love"—then wouldn't at last he long for a surprise? Nonsense. Bordering on blasphemy, if not blasphemy outright. He shook his head with irritation at the thought. It wasn't just irritating. It was disquieting. He was disturbed.

He resigned at last to get out of his quarters. Get his mind on something else for a while. A sinking feeling came to his gut, and he figured he needed to get something to eat. He had been asleep for so long, after all. And so he changed his clothes and headed out the door.

The Selenium was one of two vessels in the Dominion to be equipped with graviton arrays, owing to its massive size and mission scope as a "celestial ark." This helped to alleviate the disorienting wooziness that came with the more ubiquitous spinning ring design, substituting centripetal force with real gravity, but it still didn't feel quite right. The most obvious thing was the amount of gravitational attraction. It was calibrated to Civitas Mons—the capital planet of the Dominion—and thus noticeably gave everything more weight than he was used to on either Helios 3 or Kolob 6. Likewise, his most recent stay on Solus 4 had him accustomed to a lighter gravity, nearly identical to Helios 3.

But it wasn't simply the burdensome weight of everything in this environment. It also just felt somehow less *real.* A strange kind of pulsation in his bones. Waves of vibration tingling through his flesh. Perhaps it was some psychosomatic response. A sensation or set of sensations projected onto his body with the knowledge that beyond the bottom of the ship he should be floating out there in the great dark aether without restraint. And thus this false gravity was like the floor tugging at him, pulling him down by force.

He plodded along with leaden legs through the long halls of the large ship to the nearest elevator shaft and found his way down to the mess deck. He rounded the corner through the door-less doorway into an empty dining room. Only a single mess worker stood in the room behind a long counter. Half of the trays were empty. Those that were full included pancakes, biscuits, toast, and assorted dishes he recognized as breakfast. What time was it? Only now did he think to ask. Above the counter along a long white wall was the room's only wall hanging. A simple black and white analog clock.

The clock was like much of the ship's interior. Black and white. Or at least gray and white. White walls with gray joints and the occasional exposed metal pipe running along the white ceilings. Floors of white polished panels that clicked and clacked along unseen metal joints.

According to that clock, it was almost the eighth hour of the day. The day as defined by the ship's own arbitrary time zone. Technically, the time zone was that of the city of Salem, the capital city of the capital planet. But out here—wherever that was—was bound to be so far from Civitas Mons that such a detail was irrelevant.

"Officer on deck!" the mess worker behind the counter called out with a smile.

"Heh, at ease, crewman," Tyler replied.

The worker nodded, and Tyler couldn't help but smirk. A moment of levity in an otherwise heavy morning.

"So, what can I get for you, sir?" the crewman asked.

"I think I'll have the scrambled eggs with some bacon on the side."

"Ah, the usual, eh?"

"Uh, heh, yeah… I guess so."

"Haven't seen you around here in a while."

"Hmm?" Tyler asked, genuinely confused.

The crewman seemed to ignore his question as he continued, "They shuffle us around so much, eh?"

"Right… right…"

Tyler took his modest meal and found a seat near the middle of the room. The crewman returned to the kitchen through a door to the side of the counter. There in the quiet, empty mess hall, Tyler ate in silence. Or at least he tried to. The clicking, clanging sound of his metal fork scraping against the metal plate was practically deafening in the empty silence of the hall. The sound of his own chewing started to bother him. And his food. Was the bacon always this salty and oily and charred? Upon introspection, he realized that was pretty much all bacon. In fact, that was almost a description of its defining characteristics. Did he no longer like bacon in general?

After washing down his meal with copious amounts of water, Tyler emptied his plate into the disposal and returned his tray. He had eaten less than half of it. Maybe he wasn't very hungry after all.

Tyler spent a couple of hours touring the ship. Long white hallways across many floors of the massive ship. If it weren't for the giant numerals on the walls of each floor, one could easily get lost in those halls. A boring maze of straight lines that paradoxically proved challenging on account of their identical appearance. Navigation, telemetry, crew quarters, officer quarters, engineering. The hallways all blurred together. The larger departmental spaces were more interesting, owing to their necessary complexity, but the lines leading to them were mind-numbing.

He sat for nearly half an hour in an observation deck. Personnel came and went, but he remained looking out at stars. A vast sea of stars, beautiful in its natural chaotic complexity. He would have to come back here some time, or perhaps another observation deck on the other side of the ship.

He finally returned to his own quarters and spent another hour there. Mostly reading at his workstation. Mostly just to pass the time. When it was finally lunch, he returned to the mess deck. The same locale he had visited before. Section 42, Officers' Mess Hall.

"Hey, long time, no see," Josh remarked after tapping his friend on the shoulder as they stood in line at the counter.

"Oh, hey, heh," Tyler replied. "I'm… sorry about earlier this morning. I've just been—"

"No worries, buddy. You've been through a lot, I'm sure."

"Yeah…"

Tyler picked out beans and cornbread for lunch. It was the only thing that looked remotely appetizing to him among bins of meat loaf, jello salad, and some kind of strange casse-role. Once they had their plates, they found a seat together amid the chattering crowd of men now filling the hall.

"You could… talk about it, if you wanted," Josh said, as he casually cut his meat loaf with the side of a fork.

"I… I don't know. It's a lot, you know?"

"Sure, sure. I bet. You're the first ever to return after so long. I think, before you, the record was five days. Coming out from under the veil after five *months*. That's—that's noth-ing short of a miracle, man. A real, honest-to-goodness mira-cle. The Sovereign really has something special in mind for you."

Tyler simply nodded somberly. Josh often talked this way. The Sovereign was no "respecter of persons" and yet somehow his mysterious plans always seemed to center around Josh or himself. Children could be starving to death on some criminal mining operation, but The One's hand was clearly visible in the mundane minutiae of *their* lives.

Whether it was how a chance encounter with a street performer saved Josh from visiting a brothel or how he had re-obtained a canteen his friend had stolen from him through a convoluted series of events just so he could talk to a group of strangers about The One. Through it all, these peculiar anec-dotes of curious coincidences amounted to flowing yarns, os-tensibly meant to inspire an attitude of gratitude. And in that they were innocuous enough. Yet bubbling beneath was a fes-tering pool of pride.

The paradox of it all is that it could be pointed out—even preemptively acknowledged—and yet that only buried the pride deeper and darker. "I am simply a vessel," but oh what a vessel indeed. One on the top shelf. Not that such placement was deserved, but then no one really "deserved" anything at all, so in a sense everyone deserved whatever they got. And so to be shown such favor, to be of "the elect," the chosen few…

Tyler shook the line of thought away. He would have to unravel it another time. For now Josh was saying something, and he would have to tune back in, since he had for a moment tuned out.

"So that's why he's undergoing ablution tomorrow."

"I'm sorry, who again?"

"The new guy, Ed."

"Ed?" Tyler asked with furrowed brow.

"Yeah, he arrived onboard a few days ago. I met him during the reception at the officer's lounge. Seems like a great guy. Real strong believer."

Tyler looked off into the distance, lost in thought, and whispered to himself "Saints of Elwayae…"

"What's that?"

"Nothing… nothing."

"Okay… well, anyhow, it's good to have you back, man."

"Yeah…" Tyler replied with a sullen expression at odds with his own quiet affirmation, as he lethargically shoveled beans onto the cornbread.

They ate in silence for a little while. Or at least silence on their parts. All around them buzzed a chattering cacophony of voices echoing off the hard bare walls and tiled floors of the packed interior.

"We should hang out soon. Movie night is coming up in a couple days."

Tyler nodded quietly and took a small bite of his meager meal.

"Alright, well… see you at the service tomorrow?"

"Of course… yeah."

"See you then, my friend."

Tyler nodded and lifted his hand and gave a weak wave as they parted ways. Josh frowned to himself and walked away, while Tyler remained for a moment, picking at his food.

The rest of the day was uneventful. Tyler spent a few hours alone in his quarters, perusing his private library. Once or twice he visited the toilet alcove in his little cell. Chipped paint peeling next to an exposed pipe running up to a bare white sink. It made him think of lead. The preferred plumbing material of the Archaens ages ago. Now, of course, the pipe was galvanized steel, and the paint was some synthetic acrylic. Was that something he learned with Ed? Or was that some tidbit of knowledge he had acquired in the more distant past? Did it matter?

He decided to head to sleep early in the early evening— as measured by the arbitrary time onboard a ship floating in an endless night. And so he turned off the light in his little windowless room and in so doing filled it immediately with a deep darkness.

Perhaps tomorrow would be lighter…

TYLER slowly awoke in the dark. The sound of a voice in the distance. A garbled rumbling voice, indistinctly muttering something through the aural fog of a slow awakening. After lifting himself up out of bed and stumbling toward the light knob, the voice became distinct in his ears.

"…And may those in positions of leadership be rightly guided. May we hold them up and sustain them. For we know this too is your will. Anoint them with the Light's power. Guard them from all manner of murmuring, and guide their minds and hearts, even as you guide us all. May we approach our appointed leaders with a spirit of obedience, serving them even as we serve you…"

The voice continued droning in its dull, unending monotone, as Tyler rubbed his eyes and stretched. It was the morning invocation that came with the first day of the week. Service day. In another hour he would head to one of the ship's sanctums to which his section was assigned.

He slowly dressed in the dim golden brown light of the room's faux sunlight. Pulling his legs through each leg of his dress pants, one by one. Pulling each arm through his dress shirt. Fiddling with the buttons one by one. Wrapping himself up in the customary dress uniform was an arduous task.

The sanctum was larger than most spaces onboard the ship, but still fairly cramped compared to most permanent sanctuary structures on the planets of the Dominion. The moderately vaulted walls stretched up to what looked like stained-glass windows with gold trim. But the "windows" were really mass-produced cheap adhesive designs stuck to transparent light covers, and the trim looked like some kind of gold colored plastic. Behind those fake windows was fake sunlight. A light that was noticeably more yellow than gold. At least noticeable when you really looked at it.

And he did look at it. He had been in this particular sanctum dozens of times, and he had never really noticed it before, but now he could faintly make out the seams of the adhesive starting to peel on the corner of one. The design on the film was that of an abstract symbol, intended to look at once like a descending dove and an ascending fire. Its vague design now, however, reminded him of a corporate trade emblem of some sort. The kind of thing one might see stamped on a consumer good. The association with the mundane made him smirk briefly before he shook away the thought.

"Brother Tyler..." a rumbling voice intoned. It sent a shiver down his spine to hear it. He turned to face a man with graying hair and a small cold smile.

"Rector Falwell," Tyler replied, extended his hand, and exchanged a customary handshake.

"It is a pleasure to have you back with us."

"Yes."

"A true blessing. After so long and yet here you are. Sound of body… and sound of mind."

Tyler simply nodded as the frosty-haired man narrowed his wrinkled eyes and shot a piercing stare into Tyler's eyes, darted back and forth, examining him closely. Tyler couldn't help but gulp a little.

"When we found you, your spirit was in dire straights. It made me so sorrowful to see. But praise be to the One. The veil was lifted without any complications. And I trust that now that you have returned to the light, you see more clearly."

"Yes, yes indeed…" Tyler replied. The rector was darting around in his eyes again, and he felt the need to say something. He felt those lingering eyes like a hot spotlight. He was under examination and if he wanted the heat to go away he needed to find the right words for the rector. Quickly he found those words and recited them back to his examiner: "We see through a glass, darkly; but then face to face. Now I know in part, but then I shall know just as I also am known."

"Ah, well said. Well said…" the old man replied with a smile. Wider than before, but still cold as ever. Tyler seemed to pass his test, at least for the time being. The old man averted his eyes for a moment in thought before returning them back to Tyler, less intense now as he continued. "A debriefing has been arranged for tomorrow at the tenth hour. Operations observation deck, section six, level one, room six. I trust you will be able to attend."

"Yes sir."

"Very good. You will see the appointment reminder appear on your console. Don't be late."

"Yes sir."

The rector plastered on a wider grin, truly trying to convey some measure of warmth, but somehow failing. "A real blessing, Brother Tyler. Truly a miracle."

With that, the rector patted Tyler's shoulders and proceeded on his way. When he was several rows of seats away, Tyler breathed a sigh of relief.

Tyler navigated a sea of smiles and obligatory handshakes while making his way to a suitable seat. A couple folks actually recognized him and expressed how much of a "miracle" it was that he had returned, but most of the crowd were effectively strangers to him now. And it wasn't simply on account of different crew rotations. Some of the faces came with a vague mutual recognition, but still only a face. How many of these men had Tyler seen for months or even years throughout his tenure and never really got to know any of them? How many had never bothered to get to know *him*? Everyone was a "brother" but that was little more than a title. Genuine friendships were few and far between. How strange to be in such close proximity to others and yet be more distant than the stars.

A moment or two after Tyler found his seat, a man climbed the steps of the raised platform at the front of the sanctum. The man sat down at a keyboard synthesizer off to one side away from the lectern at the center and started to play a tinkling piano melody on its keys. That was everyone's cue to find their seats, and within a few minutes everyone was seated.

After a few more minutes of playing, a gray-haired man slowly climbed the steps and turned toward the seated crowd as he stood behind the lectern. It was the rector.

"Good morning, brothers!"

"Good morning," came a rumbling reply in unison from the crowd.

"In the writings we read that a man of The One must be fully equipped for every good deed," the rector stated and paused before continuing. "This morning, I hope you have all equipped yourself with forks and knives for breakfast, because we have quite the spiritual feast prepared."

A murmur arose of a few nervous chuckles scattered sparsely throughout the sanctum, mostly from newcomers who hadn't heard the rector's stale old line which he had used on occasion at least a dozen times before. Tyler winced at the words and looked side to side to gauge how everyone else was reacting. Was he alone in cringing? If he wasn't, he couldn't tell. All the men around him sat with mostly blank expressions.

"Our dear brother, Reverend Campbell, will be delivering today's address entitled 'Lean not unto thine own understanding.' But before we begin, let us sing praises unto the Sovereign together."

As the rector quietly exited the platform, words appeared to either side of the stage and the lone man playing his modest synthesizer started to play accompanying music to the tune of "Onward, Kyrian Warrior."

After the song, the reverend stepped up to the platform and delivered an opening prayer before launching into a rambling lecture on the value of "trust" over and counter to reason. As Tyler listened intently to a talk covering a topic which he had heard dozens of times in the past, it was as though he was hearing it fresh for the first time. It was like receiving laser corrective surgery after having myopia for years. The old fuzzy thoughts he received from the platform were coming into sharp focus. He couldn't help but apply a critical lens to them and see them for what they were.

At one point the speaker had stated "...by this private reasoning, by deferring to so called 'logic' and 'evidence' many have sadly been led astray." This translated in Tyler's mind to "your own mind cannot be trusted, set critical thinking aside and simply accept whatever we tell you to think." Could that really be what they were effectively implying? How absurd was that? If one couldn't trust one's own thoughts, how could one trust the thoughts of someone else? Wouldn't it require a mental process to come to the conclusion that the thoughts of someone else were trustworthy?

Precisely. That was Ed's voice. It came into his imagination, and a part of him shuddered at its presence. Yet, he couldn't help but hold to this line of reasoning. It was all too clear to him now. And Ed would be the first one to say something like, "Hey, don't take my word for it." He could reject Ed personally and everything he stood for, but still find himself agreeing whenever it made sense. To do otherwise would be the essence of the ad hominem fallacy.

The disconcertingly disagreeable oration finally ended after half an hour or so. It came as a relief.

"Finally, before we close, brothers, a new crewman has come into our fold. One Crewman Edmund Young. Mister Young has only recently moved into the realm of our Sovereign's Dominion, having lived until now amidst the fallen stars. His dedication to our cause is already readily apparent, but he wishes to symbolize this by undergoing ablution today."

With those words a young man stepped from behind a recessed wall behind the speaker. A young man that looked he could have been a teenager, wearing a long white robe. He waded into a small pool of water behind a clear half wall and smiled and waved at the crowd. His smile dropped and his hand slowly retreated as someone to his left muttered something.

Young, indeed, Tyler thought.

Into the pool of water waded another man, also dressed in a long white robe. It was the rector.

"Do you recognize that there are no gods—there is only The One—and that the Meshek is his Messenger?" the rector intoned, his voice booming throughout the sanctum's hidden audio system.

"I do."

"Will you commit yourself to the Sovereign's will, expanding his dominion across any and all institutions foreign and domestic?"

"I will."

"Then I immerse you in the name of the Old, the Young, and the Light."

With that, the aging rector dunked the young man under the water and immediately drew him out like a dumpling being dipped in a condiment bowl.

"I am proud to present to you, brothers, our dear brother in Meshek... Brother Young!"

The crowd erupted into applause. But as Tyler look around, there were no real smiles. Occasional nods and whispering asides. But no real excitement or visible happiness. The applause was merely... obligatory.

After a final song that dragged on for far too long, Tyler quickly made his way to the sanctum doors. But before he could completely make his exit, he was caught.

"Chris!" a voice called out from the crowd.

"Oh... hey, Josh."

"Trying to leave without catching up with your best friend?"

"Heh..." Tyler simply responded. How could he tell him that the answer to that question was effectively "Yes?"

"Hey, so Mike and I are thinking of meeting up at Luigi's for lunch. Wanna join us?"

"Luigi's? I don't know…" Tyler replied hesitantly. The prospect of hooking up a nutrient bag and eating in neurospace wasn't exactly appealing to him. At least not anymore. Did he really use to "eat" that way all the time?

"C'mon, man, you know it's better than the mess deck. Especially on the first day of the week. Would you rather have a tuna sandwich?"

A stale tuna sandwich or a nutrient bag coordinated with virtual dining. Now that he was reminded of his choices, he was torn.

"Uh… ugh… okay. Sure."

"Cool beans, man. See you in neuro."

He spent an hour or two at the virtual cafe inside neurospace. Once he started eating, the tastes and sensations were very well done and better than he remembered. Nevertheless, he couldn't help thinking about the nutrient bag he had sent over the vacuum tube to his room, presently dripping down his unconscious throat somewhere back in the real world.

After some thought, what he was really dreading after all more than the dining experience was the prospect of prolonged conversation. Fortunately, he managed to stay quiet and blend into the virtual wall of the virtual dining room and remain mostly unmolested. His uncharacteristic behavior was briefly noted by Josh, but he and Mike quickly moved onto conversing amongst themselves with two or three other men that tagged along.

The rest of the day, Tyler spent roaming the halls of the ship again. He went wherever he could find quiet. Wherever he could be alone with his thoughts. Paradoxically, he was growing increasingly lonely, but he knew that wouldn't go away by spending time with any of his old comrades. There were others he was missing now. Ed and Frank and Julio. But most of all he missed Anne. But that also brought him guilt and confusion. What could he make about what he did—how he lived—for those months? A part of him felt it was something worthy of confession. Yet another part couldn't really see why. And that latter part was growing stronger with every passing hour.

At last, he retired for the night, but left the light on as he did. Somehow that dim golden light brought him some measure of comfort. It somehow made him feel a little less lonesome as he drifted off to sleep.

WHEN Tyler awoke, the room was filled with a slightly blue-tinged silvery gray light. Had he adjusted the color temperature in his sleep? He slowly arose and fiddled with the knob, pushing it in to adjust the color, but it remained the same. Odd.

He flipped open his console screen and was immediately greeted with an announcement. Apparently, a systems malfunction was impacting lighting systems throughout the ship. Lighting was still functional, so it was given a low priority for repair. There was also a reminder on his calendar. In three hours he would have a meeting with Rector Falwell and probably several others. He was not looking forward to it.

After he got dressed and stepped into the hall, he was bathed in that same blue-tinged silvery gray light as in his room. It was a strange, eerie glow, but somehow a nice change of pace. The halls were emptier than usual compared to the day prior, when crew shifts were arranged so that everyone was able to attend service at different times.

He roamed the halls, casually exploring areas he normally never visited. The silver-blue light reminded him of something. Something from the depths of his past. Walking barefoot outdoors in the crisp air of a chill night. A bright moonlit night on the world of his birth.

The memory was rich, and in the midst of recollection he could almost feel the sensation of soft earth against his feet and tufts of grass between his toes. His brother was there with him. A real brother. Brothers by flesh and blood. That was before they grew up and parted ways. And his heart grew heavy remembering how that happened. A year or two after his parents divorced, his brother gave up on Kyrianism all together. When he was fourteen and his brother Eric was nineteen, he moved with his mother to Kolob 6, a world at the edge of the Dominion. Eric stayed behind.

When Jonah turned twenty, the Dominion claimed the Kolob system. His mother fled back to Helios 3 and rejoined his brother, but he decided to stay and welcome the regime change. A good deal of debates, often heated, ensued between him and his mother for several weeks before she left. She had stayed right until the bitter end, trying whatever she could to convince him to flee with her. But he was a zealot and had been rooting for the Dominion for two or three years prior. When she left on the last available transport, troops landed on Kolob 6 the very next day.

It was his mother that called him "Jonah." A name she said with such affection. It in turn came to inspire in him an awkward bitterness. And thus, when he introduced himself for the first time at the Crusader Academy on Civitas Mons, he gave his name as "Chris."

His mind was called back to the present now when he passed an open doorway along one of the silver halls through which he was aimlessly meandering. He stepped back and peered through the open door to see rows of men lying side by side on flat cushioned gurneys. After half a moment, he recalled what he was seeing. Neurolab. It was for those low-ranking enlisted men who were not afforded the luxury of having a neurospace terminal in their own quarters.

In a matter of days, that would be him. In his own quarters, but it would make little difference. Twelve hours of neurospace a day, day after day. That was the average working shift in signals intelligence. Only interrupted by occasional bathroom and meal breaks. Of course, with urinal/rectal attachments and nutrient bags, some of the men opted to just spend all day in neuro uninterrupted—even after their shift was over.

"Is there something I can do for you, sir?" a man behind an administrative desk asked. It was the chief petty officer in charge of the lab. Tyler had been standing at the doorway, staring in for a lingering moment.

"Uh... no, no. Carry on, Chief."

The man behind the desk nodded his head and Tyler shuffled away. As he ambled along, he tried to think of places on the ship he hadn't visited to date. That's when it came to him. He had visited a number of observation decks, but always on the starboard side. Perhaps a view from the other side of the ship might be a change. He wasn't familiar enough with astronomy to pick out constellations, but perhaps he might spot some differences nevertheless.

As he sauntered through the long white aisles bathed in silver blue light, it felt like he was meandering through a dream. His surroundings were as surreal as they were empty. Most of the crew was effectively dreaming, away on cushioned platforms. Cushions that weren't as comfortable as back on the station, but bed-like nonetheless.

When he stepped through the sliding door of a port-side observation room, what confronted him was more surreal than anything he had experienced this strange day. He literally had to ask himself if he were dreaming. He rubbed his eyes and looked again, and it was still there. There in the observation deck out amongst the stars was a blue-green marble, hanging there like an unusually large and colorful moon.

There were half a dozen or so men in the room, which was a little unusual for a single observation deck as small as this particular room. Similar spaces on the starboard side were rarely that populated, but then it made sense considering the more interesting view out to the planet in the distance. Of course, then when he thought about it, why wouldn't there be even more men in these spaces? Considering how crew shifts were staggered, there were still plenty of men off duty at this hour. But then he remembered neurospace. Considering how even the men who spent all day in neurospace as part of their regular duties continued to *indulge* even after hours, it would be the case all the more for those men who actually had duties outside of neuro.

"Excuse me, Ensign," Tyler said as he tapped a younger man on the shoulder.

"Yes, sir?"

"What is our present position?"

"I'm afraid I don't recall the exact coordinates, sir. I work in Telemetry. The Astrometry lab would—"

"I don't need precise coordinates. Just… *that…*" Tyler said, pointing at the large orb looming in the window. "What planet is that?"

The ensign gave Tyler a puzzled look. "Solus 4, sir. Did you recently transfer, sir?"

"Something like that…" he remarked quietly, shifting his eyes to the distance and darting them from side to side. "Thank you."

The ensign nodded in turn, and Tyler continued staring at the planet in quiet awe.

"I can introduce you to her," a man along the rear wall remarked to another.

"Keep it down, man!" the other exclaimed in a hushed tone.

"You want the prog or not?"

"Yeah yeah, let's talk about it in neuro."

"Dude, nobody cares."

"Whatever, just c'mon…" the other remarked and then ushered the other out of the room.

Tyler shook his head at the exchange. Virtual women. The digital chattel of sexually repressed men with raging libidos. Their proliferation and usage was something of a public secret. While deemed inappropriate, it was a minor transgression that largely went ignored. At least when the software was *women*.

But while in the past he would have turned a blind eye and then felt guilt—always guilt—since he himself had made his own clandestine procurement, now he thought instead about how absurd it all was. A perfectly understandable outlet for natural longings in a very unnatural environment. A ship full of young men, completely barren of women. What else should they do?

Julio. The reminder made his blood run cold. How would *his* own natural longings be treated? He shuddered at the thought. And like the day before, the incongruity was crystal clear. A very disconcerting clarity. He shook the thought away. The debriefing was in less than an hour now. He should probably start heading that way.

Ship section six. First floor. Room six. When the door slid open to the room, a shudder slithered down his spine. It was the same room where he had awakened in darkness two days ago. The room was lit up now, covered in that silver blue light, like everywhere else. Being on the starboard side, the field of stars outside the large window panes lacked the blue moon which loomed large in the stars of the port side.

He turned to his right to see three men seated at a table along the far wall. In the center sat his commanding officer, Commander Cathcart—a man he hardly ever saw but once a month at most. To his superior's right sat some man he had never met, and to his left was the rector. The room was smaller than he recalled, and the gurney was gone, but a general sense of unease lingered nonetheless.

"Lieutenant Tyler, right on time," Cathcart remarked. "If you'd like to make your way to the bench, we can begin. This shouldn't take very long."

"Yes sir," Tyler replied with a salute and made his way to the center of the room. The door slid shut behind him. The three men all kept their gazes locked on him as he approached. The only thing this chamber of stars lacked was a spotlight. He felt very much on the spot, nevertheless.

A little over a quarter of an hour of questions. But strangely, all focused almost exclusively on the events leading up to the explosion and subsequent crash of the Pescha. It wasn't completely strange, of course. That merited some measure of inquiry. But it was technically a civilian ship. It seemed more of a subject for criminal investigation than military intelligence.

"That should be all," his commanding officer finally said. "Thank you, Lieutenant. Was there anything else you'd like to add?"

"Nothing regarding the Pescha, but..."

"Yes?"

"I was gone for over five months. You… never asked me anything about Talos Mystico."

"Talos what?"

"The station. The place I lived for nearly half a year."

"I don't see how it's particularly relevant to *this* hearing."

"Is there not any strategic interest regarding the station? Or any concern about their particular discoveries?"

"Like what specifically?"

"Well, for one, I know the station is presently investigating ancient ruins and the biological remains of some manner of purported alien civilization. Possibly even contemporary. If there's any validity to their claims, it seems like something meriting analysis. Probably not a threat assessment, but some manner of—"

"Brother Tyler," the rector interjected, "how could there possibly be any validity to such claims?"

Tyler swallowed before replying, "I'm not implying there is, of course. But hypothetically the ramifications… I mean… purely from a missionary perspective there may be, uh, reason to investigate. A whole new people that might need to hear—"

"People…?"

"The native inhabitants—hypothetical native inhabitants."

"Distortion and falsehood," the rector remarked while shaking his head. "It would be a waste of valuable time and resources to even bother giving a second thought to such absurdities."

"Right… yes, of course."

Commander Cathcart breathed out and stretched in the midst of the ensuing silence before saying "Very well, then, if that is all gentlemen—"

"Considering the potential gravity of such distortion and falsehood," Tyler interjected as he lifted his eyes back from the floor, "would it be prudent to target this station for eradication?"

"And how much *gravity* do you think such distortion really has?" the rector asked as he cocked his head to one side.

"From what I saw during my stay, it could… prove quite misleading."

"Brother Tyler, what you've gone through while under the veil is extraordinary to say the least. And no one here blames you for your state of mind under such a state. This is a debriefing, not an inquisition. That being said, I think you must take into account that you clearly did not have your full faculties of reason at your disposal while under the veil. If you had, you clearly would have seen how unconvincing and nonsensical such hogwash really was. Have no fear, the faithful will not be so easily misled. Not while those within the Sovereign's Dominion stand as sentinels against such falsehood."

"Right, of course. Thank you," Tyler replied and did his best to give a convincing soft smile. It was effective enough that he almost convinced himself.

Tyler's commanding officer spoke up again. "Thank you everyone for your time. Shall we adjourn then?"

Everyone nodded in agreement and slowly filed out of the room. The rector and Tyler were the last ones out, and as Tyler was at the door, the older man grabbed him softly by the arm and pulled him aside.

"Regarding your protracted absence, Brother Tyler," the rector said in a hushed tone, "if there's anything you'd like to talk through or discuss, please don't hesitate to visit my office. Yes?"

Tyler nodded and softly smiled. "Of course, yes, thank you."

"Good, very good," the rector remarked with a cold smile and patted his shoulder.

Tyler immediately headed back to his little alcove. Once he was inside his tiny retreat and the door closed behind him, he breathed out a long sigh and ran his fingers through his hair. The crucible was over... for now. But now he needed some answers.

He took a seat at his workstation and started searching through the ship's interdepartmental data repository. Where was he precisely? In a prograde orbit, approximately 385,000 kilometers from the surface of Solus 4. How long would they be there? Another five days. The Selenium was scheduled to depart and return farther into Dominion space at the end of the last day of the week. At the start of the next week, his medical suspension would be over, and he would be expected to resume duty.

TYLER was violently torn from sleep by a sharp blaring blast of sound accompanied by a bright red oscillating light. He quickly jumped to his feet and threw on his clothes before he remembered. Third day of the week. Emergency drill.

Outside his door in the aisle was a flurry of activity. Men briskly jogging in the flashing red light. Some men barking directions at others over the buzz saw sound of the alarm. The sight alone was enough to give him a headache, let alone the sound.

"General quarters! General quarters! All hands man battle stations!" came the drill announcement.

Tyler retreated back into his alcove with a sigh. He lied back down on his bed and closed his eyes. He would have slept if he could, but he couldn't. The sound of the alarm ceased after a couple minutes, but the pulsating red glow of his surroundings continued. So he rested there for nearly half an hour, grazing the edges of sleep without ever fully dipping in.

Once the drill was over, he decided to make his way to the closest mess deck. When he arrived, the hall was filled to the brim with personnel. He asked for his meal to go and brought it back to his quarters. These days, his hunger for solitude was insatiable. He needed time to think.

And so he took that time. After his meal, he decided he needed a change of scenery. There was a department or two he hadn't visited—at least not since this first week of his new life—but he craved a real change. A change that reviewing areas of the ship couldn't provide.

He had been reluctant to drop into neurospace for some time. His visit to "Luigi's" a couple days prior came with a reluctance not solely felt on account of the nutrient bag. It was also a matter of simply longing to stay connected. He felt the need to stay grounded. To keep his feet firmly planted in reality. But that necessity was starting to fade and a greater need took its place. He needed answers. Or at least conclusions.

When he dropped in, he was on the inside of a large white cube. The constructor canvas. The glaring artificiality of its bland white walls was unnerving. It reminded him too much of the world he was looking to escape.

"System load new environment."

A floating translucent panel appeared in front of him with a series of animated thumbnails. Each one depicted a recently used environment in his own personal history. A seedy alleyway from a crime drama. A domed arena for a shooting game. A set of simple abstract floating polygons used as platforms for a puzzle game. A patient room inside a hospital, with a flirtatious busty nurse prominently jiggling in the thumbnail.

"Ugh…" he groaned to himself, as he swiped past all of it with his index finger. He scrolled down to ambient historic simulations. One thumbnail in particular caught his eye. A rocky outcropping in the middle of what looked like a forested area near an ancient city. The title text read "Collis Martis."

After he tapped the thumbnail, it expanded into view all around him. He slowly circled around and took in his new environment. He was atop the craggy limestone hill in the thumbnail, and from it, he could see all manner of structures in the distance beyond the immediate greenery at the base of the outcropping. Atop another prominent outcropping in the distance to his right, he could see an ancient building outlined with columns.

"Heh…" he laughed to himself. As it turned out, it was the ancient city of Minerva. He looked down at his feet. *And that would make* this *Tyr's Rock.*

His smile faded as he was reminded of this place's particular significance. "Usal…" he whispered to himself. He looked around the hill again, imagining Usal talking with the philosophers of the day, telling them about The One. The unknown one.

"For in him we live, and move, and have our being…" he recalled to himself. Words Usal had lifted from a pagan poet. Words originally referring to a god. But Usal had instead applied them to The One.

How many other things had Kyrianism appropriated? From the very beginning, it was taking things. Ideas, cultures, traditions, people. All of them swirled up in the whirlwind as it marched along under the banner of the divided eye. The eye that runs to and fro. The eye in every place beholding evil and good. The eye that sits over the righteous, but turns in wrath against the wicked.

And so everywhere Kyrianism marched, it gobbled up diversity and left division in its wake. It was in the attributed words of the Meshek. "I came not to send peace, but a sword."

Tyler shook his head at the thought. *The division was an inevitability of a necessarily divisive message.*

Are you so sure its divisiveness was necessary? The voice of Ed. It came into his mind, and its vividness shook him for a moment.

He replied in his head with his own interior voice, debating with the phantom Ed of his imagination. *People don't want the truth. Speak truth and you will encounter resistance. That's just how it is.*

What about truths upon which most people can agree? Surely you can think of some.

Convenient truths, perhaps. Truths which do not call for people to change their course of action.

Are you comfortable changing your course of action?

That question echoing in his mind gave him some serious pause for thought. Was he ready to change? Was he strong enough to make any necessary sacrifices to live in accordance with the truth? Even if that meant abandoning or even subsequently *denying* things which he held to be true in the past?

Hypothetically, yes. He reminded himself about how he had been raised in a sect that he abandoned. "End Day Arrivalism." It wasn't too dissimilar to Ed's own "Saints of Elwayae." Less informed people commonly confused the two, in fact.

I've changed before. I've sacrificed to be where I am now.

Life is about continual *change.* Continual *sacrifice. If you're not dying, you're not living. Resting comfortably in your present belief. That's the true second death.*

Perhaps, but only where death is needed. The fire may burn off the dross, and yet the gold remains. It would be foolish to toss out the gold.

Don't toss out the baby with the bath water, eh? Just be sure it's truly a baby in that bath water and not a lead idol.

That would only weigh you down. Test all things and hold on to what is fine—but only what is fine.

Tyler nodded to himself. It was a fair point.

Tyler continued debating like this with himself for the better part of an hour as he sat atop the lonely rock, watching the trees of the forest sway in the wind. He then decided to climb down the hill and tour the trees below. He spent close to an hour appreciating the woods. Even if it was simulated, it was the closest thing he would have to a natural landscape.

"I used to think it was nothing but folly to trust my feelings. Pure objective reasoning was all that I needed. But without feelings—emotive inclinations, intuitive judgments, whatever you want to call it—upon what basis could I possibly reason? Pure deduction is only as valid as its premises."

Another snippet of a half-remembered rant from Ed. He had a retort in mind. *Ah, but the heart is deceitful above all things, who can know it?*

The imagined reply came quickly. *You must love The One with all your heart, and by your love will you be known. Is that not the heart of Kyrianism?*

Very true, but that is why we must receive a new heart.

And how will you know when you have received it?

The evidence we can see in our lives. The new man…

But then he realized he was starting to recite old rhetoric to himself. It wasn't completely honest.

You know the truth. To judge such evidence, one would need to consult the heart.

So what's your solution?

But he knew what he would say to that too.

My solution? Who says there's a problem? We have good inclinations and bad inclinations. This isn't a defect. It's simply something fundamental to the universe. 'I create light and I create darkness.' The sooner we make peace with that and stop fighting against our own inclinations and instead recognize their need for direction, the sooner we can be our own shepherd. Direct the beast within.*

How can I trust myself over The One…?

But he knew the answer to that one before the thought even fully formed. It was the same answer he had days prior at the service. The answer could itself be stated as a question: What would be the effective difference if he had to trust himself enough to determine whether whatever guidance he might receive from The One was from The One in the first place?

And then words from another voice came to his mind. The words of one of his favorite authors and Kyrian thinkers. "The Sovereign whispers in our desires and speaks in our conscience…"[3]

His conscience. Of course. He would always do well to listen to it, regardless of the consequences. Regardless of its demands. That was the voice he would choose to obey. What did his conscience tell him today?

He decided he should get back to the real world. Reality, after all, was worth embracing, whatever the cost. Even when it was painful. And with that, the rest of the quote came to him: "…but shouts in our pain." He nodded somberly to himself. He finally fully admitted it to himself: Something was deeply wrong.

Tyler went to the mess deck to grab lunch. There he ran into Josh again.

"Hey man, did you hear the latest from the Confederation?" Josh asked as they took their seats together in the crowded mess hall.

"Can't say I have."

"They passed a whole 'resolution' issuing a proclamation condemning the Kyrian Dominion and what they're calling 'child marriage.' Such a load of horse shit."

"Child marriage…?"

"Yeah," Josh scoffed. "They're claiming our breast test is a barbaric measure of marriageability. That 'girls under fifteen are incapable of legal consent.' As though they have any moral ground to stand on. Whole Confederation is filled with fucking faggots."

Tyler winced at Josh's words. One word in particular, in fact. He didn't use the word routinely, but whenever Josh said that one word, it always made Tyler a little uncomfortable. But now, he felt something stronger. He reflected on it for a second or two while Josh was wagging his head. Incensed. That's what he felt. Incensed.

"You shouldn't say that."

"Say what?"

"That word. It's… it's needlessly insulting and demeaning."

"What word? 'Faggot?'"

Tyler winced again and nodded his head.

"I'm just calling it like it is, man. I know it's strong language and all I guess, but I mean, what these people do… it's —"

"They're still people, aren't they?" Tyler asked, his heart starting to race at the growing confrontation.

"Well, yeah, sure. But I'm just saying that—"

"And doesn't the Sovereign love them too?"

Josh frowned and then coughed nervously. "Well, okay… Anyways, umm, hey I missed you at movie night last night."

Tyler sighed and looked down. "Yeah. I… haven't been feeling too well lately, I guess."

"Right, sure sure… I'm all ears any chance we can get. You know me."

Tyler nodded his head, his eyes still averted. After a moment, he looked back at his old friend and spoke. "Josh… what are we doing out here?"

"We're out on patrol. Whole ship got diverted just to pick you up. I'm not sure why we haven't departed yet, actually. Above our pay grade, I guess."

Tyler shook his head. "That's not what I mean."

"What *do* you mean, Chris?"

"Just this… perpetual fighting. We're always on patrol. Always gathering intelligence. What's the new sector we can expand into? What's the new territory we can claim? We've basically been at war—one kind or another—for… for so long…"

"Man, I hear you. We both could use a long vacation."

Tyler sighed. "No, I mean… in general. The Dominion. Since before I received ablution. You were born in the Dominion and there was fighting then."

Josh nodded his head. "We can never be at peace in this world. A world that hates the Sovereign. Whenever we lose heart, we just have to remember this isn't our home. But one day we'll be called home. And as long as we fight the good fight, the Sovereign won't forget that."

"How do you know that's true? How do you know we're not all just being… being used. I was raised in a heretical sect that would have made the same claim."

"Heh, yeah, and that's the damnable thing about these sects, man. It's counterfeit Kyrianism. Revelle knows how to really mislead the masses. Just get close enough to the truth, but then twist it. The Rascal cannot make, only mock."

Tyler sighed again. A larger sigh now. He wasn't getting through. It almost seemed pointless. And then there was a looming fear. He could feel the lingering stares of eyes around the room. Men glancing out of the corner of their eyes and whispering.

"I don't know, Josh," Tyler finally said. "It just seems like maybe there could be a better way."

Josh frowned and glanced off to the side, before returning his gaze. "You're not… I mean, if I didn't know better it almost sounds like you're thinking of going ten or something, heh…" Josh chuckled nervously in an attempt to soften the blow of such a suggestion.

If only Josh knew what was going on through his head. The suggestion of "going ten"—of expressing pessimistic dissent—that would have been an understatement. What Tyler was contemplating was more along the lines of desertion, if not outright treason.

"No, just… never mind," Tyler said at last.

"Heh, yeah, uh, anyways… I guess I should get back to my shift here soon."

Tyler nodded.

"See you around, man."

"See you around…"

After they parted ways, Tyler decided to explore one area of the ship he hadn't visited yet. Magazine Operations. It was a long ride down to near the bottom of the ship. The strange vibrating pulsation in his flesh was all the stronger, the closer he got to the ship's graviton array along the ship's keel.

A whole network of iron pipes ran along the ceiling toward the center of the room as he entered. The technicians barely acknowledged his presence as he toured the industrial space. In the center was the reactor, sealed off by transparent walls encircling it, available only to authorized reactor room workers.

Inside that reactor was magnetically suspended plasma. It was similar to the larger fusion reactor elsewhere on the ship in Engineering. But this reactor served only one purpose: War. It fueled the plasma canons on the ship.

Glancing up at that network of tubes racing along in assorted directions, Tyler shook his head and whispered, "Not anymore."

THE next day in the morning, after breakfast, Tyler immediately headed to the ship library. He had solid concerns and solid questions. Now he needed solid answers.

The little library was as quaint as it was small. A carpeted floor and acoustic panels helped reduce the ambient noise of the foot traffic elsewhere on deck and general rumbles of the ship overall. Over half of the library's space was dedicated to a series of desks for workstations lower ranking crewmen could use. Considering only half of the personnel on the ship were part of the Kalevite order, there were a lot of men who had no access to neurospace. These workstations were their only real source of entertainment outside of playing cards or drinking beer.

"Can I help you, sir?" the petty officer behind the desk asked as he walked in.

"Uh, yes, I'm looking to review a copy of The Institutes of Libbenical Law."

"Author?"

"Shroudnoy."

"I can send you over a digital copy to your terminal if you'd li—"

"I'd like to review a physical copy if I could, actually."

"Uh, sure, let me… just check…" the attendant said as he scrolled down the screen at his desk. "We do have a copy. Only one copy. It's in the relics section, actually, heh. I'll just have to get my gloves, sir."

Tyler nodded as the man reached under the desk and rummaged through a couple boxes and retrieved a pair of white cotton gloves.

"If you'll follow me, sir."

The attendant escorted Tyler to a small bookshelf at the very back of the room housing a locked glass case. After unlocking the case, the attendant handed Tyler a pair of gloves and prompted him to put them on.

"Here we are, sir," the man said as he lifted the lofty tome onto a nearby pedestal. A massive blue book with gold lettering.

"Thank you," Tyler replied.

"As a reference work, this would need to stay in the library. But if you'd like, feel free to take it with you to a seat. Although… it looks like you're going to need a desk to hold it, heh. And gloves on, of course."

"Could I reserve a time at a workstation, actually?"

"Uh, sure. There will probably be a bit of a wait though, sir."

"I understand, that's fine."

The man nodded and walked off back to his desk. Tyler started to slowly turn through the pages as he tried to recall a specific passage of text he had in mind. Upon turning the pages, he remembered it had been quite a while since he handled a real physical book. In fact, the only time he had in years was… back in Ed's office at Talos Mystico.

The thought prompted him to raise his eyes and take a look around. The little minimalist shelves behind him. The simple glaring white lights in the ceiling. The space was surrealistically boring. It lacked any of the grandeur and mystique that came to him when he thought of the word "library." In many ways, the library he had made in neurospace somehow seemed more real, paradoxically enough. The wafting clouds of incense. The stone shelves. The natural sunlight. It all seemed more fitting. More like a *real* library than this artificial little space he was in now.

He had to wait more than half an hour to get a seat at a workstation. And the attendant made a point of telling him that that was surprisingly quick for most days. Considering the demand, there could often be a wait of two or three hours.

Once he was seated, Tyler made the best use of his hour-long reservation. Combing through digital resources at the workstation. Rapidly flipping through the ancient tome. Comparing it with the text on the terminal. Making notes on screen as he went.

After his hour was up, he carefully handed the tome back to the attendant, along with the gloves, and immediately jogged out of the room and briskly marched back to his quarters. His mind was racing faster than his feet. And he was really getting somewhere.

He spent several more hours through the morning researching furiously on the workstation in his little alcove. He skipped lunch all together. He was too immersed to even notice.

Three hours into the afternoon, he finally stopped. With a slow nod, he whispered to himself, "Flawed at the core." The external acknowledgment sent a shiver down his spine. To hear those words on his own lips with his own voice. It came as a shock.

But then he recalled something Ed had said once months ago…

"You probably won't understand this precisely now, but knowledge and experience not only shapes people—it can also wall them off. Once they believe they have figured it all out, acquired a worldview and come to trust their choices to an overarching meta-narrative, anything which questions that set of operating premises is perceived as a nuisance—if not an outright threat."

He hadn't understood then, but he understood now. All that time he spent with Ed. Every day in Ed's office, listening to him in between work. It wasn't incidental. It wasn't simply finding him something to do at the station. It was Ed's plan all along.

But he didn't feel manipulated. Ed could have told him nothing but one-sided narratives and inculcated him with propaganda. But he didn't. Instead, he was really quite fair—charitable even. And that made his insights and critical thinking irrefutable.

Thank you, Dr. Reed.

At that same moment, a chime sounded on his system, and he bolted up in his chair. For a fraction of a second a sharp fear came upon him as though he was noticed. Caught in the midst of dangerous thinking. Reason quickly returned, however. He had simply received a messaging alert. It was a reminder about an appointment in a couple hours with Healing Hands.

At the time of his appointment, Tyler made his way to Healing Hands. A simple medical bay, as colorless as it was clinically clean. Not terribly different than the rest of the ship in that respect really, but perhaps slightly more so. He was reminded of the examination room back on Talos Mystico. The large window looking out on an open field past the tree line. But here there was only barren white walls.

"Ah, Lieutenant Tyler, right on time. If you'll follow me…"

The medic led him to a gatch bed, attached to which was a familiar shelled out tube encircling the top of the bed for his head. A sense of dread came over him. He slid his head inside that cylindrical enclosure as instructed, after some brief hesitation that went unnoticed by the medic. When he was eleven years old, a couple of boys at his school had locked him in a utility closet. Fifteen agonizing minutes went by until he was discovered. He had dealt privately with anxiety toward enclosed spaces for years since.

As the medic performed a scan with the scanning apparatus, he was reminded of his first time meeting Ed. Was it simple unease he had felt then? Or was it some unconscious holdover of his past trauma? Perhaps the emotional residue of a memory that was otherwise blocked. In any case, his anxiety was lessened then, and thinking back on the experience gave him some measure of comfort in the present. Effectively, his experience in Ed's office functioned as a kind of incidental exposure therapy—the kind of thing in retrospect he needed but had never previously received.

"Everything looks good here," the medic explained. "You can come out now. We'll just take some vitals, and you should be all set."

The medic washed his hands and returned. He then pressed his fingers against Tyler's wrist for a minute as he looked at his wristwatch. He then jotted down some notes and repeated the process, this time counting Tyler's breaths.

"Place this under your tongue, please," the medic said, handing Tyler a thermometer. He had never really thought about it before, but every experience he had with "Healing Hands" in the past had been similarly manual. Back at the station, his vitals would have been assessed with a specialized medical polyscan. Here, on the other hand, he was holding in his mouth a glass tube filled with mercury, handed to him by a man wearing a wristwatch. Everything about it was very strangely antiquated.

When he thought about it, the oral thermometer seemed to encapsulate the entire paradox of the Selenium, and in turn perhaps the Dominion as a whole. Technology was merely a means to an end. In fact, everything was a means to an end. Whether it was technology employed purely for war or cheap art and music produced purely for propaganda. A quote came to Tyler's mind: "It regarded intelligence simply and solely as a weapon… Thought was for it a device necessary to certain ends, but thought in itself did not interest it."[4]

The original antecedent of that "it" was something infernal. To see how "it" applied to the Dominion and its practices or Kyrian apologetics in general… it gave him a shudder.

"Alright, you should be all set. Just come back in a couple of days for a follow-up check, and assuming all goes well, you can return to duty next week."

Tyler nodded quietly in response. The man made his remark as though it was good news. Yet to Tyler it was only a reminder of his limited time.

"Oh, and Commander Cathcart sent a note that you are to report to the brig once we're done here."

"The brig?"

"That's what it says, yeah. I'm guessing it's not for an extended stay, otherwise they would have sent a security escort," the medic remarked with a chuckle.

Tyler made his way down to the bottom of the ship. Those same subtle isochronic undulations pulsated in his flesh, heightening his unease. Why the brig?

"Ah, Lieutenant Tyler. Thank you for joining us," Cathcart said in greeting, as Tyler entered the brig. It was a simple space with white walls. About as bland and boring as the rest of the ship. No more nor less.

"I came as soon as I was informed, sir," Tyler replied. Once he did, he slowly glanced around the room and took in the space. Standing next to his commanding officer was a man he didn't recognize. He wore a stern expression and stood with his arms folded behind his back.

"This shouldn't take very long, Lieutenant. Please come in," Cathcart said, as he gestured Tyler to step closer toward the control station at the center of the room.

As he did, Tyler could see more of the cell to his left. A transparent wall with a locked transparent sliding door to one side. Within that cell was a man. An older man. A balding head with faint wisps of hair faced him, as the man rested his head on one hand, staring at the floor. Two legs spread far apart in a casual stance. Two legs which Tyler could see were made of metal. Crude skeletal metal limbs attached to his knees.

The man looked up as Tyler entered, showing him a grizzled face filled with gray stubble. The familiarity of that face shocked him to the core.

"Well, if it isn't Johnny boy," the man remarked.

"Do you recognize this man?" Cathcart asked.

"I, uh… yes, I do, sir," Tyler answered.

"A Mister William J. Evans. According to our records, he served in the Engineering section of the MS Pescha, Telecommunications Department," Cathcart explained.

"And you, Lieutenant Tyler," the stern man spoke up, "are listed a number of times on incident records assigned to this man. Can you explain the nature of these incident reports?"

Tyler looked over to the older man in the cell, locked eyes for a moment, before the man averted his glance and shook his head dismissively. Seeing this man before him caused Tyler's curious double vision to return. On the one hand, this was the man he met in the dark. The man who gave him some measure of guidance. The man whom he mourned. On the other hand, this was a man he called to his personal quarters multiple times to investigate a spotty network connection. A man who introduced himself, but he never bothered to recall his name. He thought it was something with a "B." He viewed the man at the time as a menial worker there to provide him service. Service with which he was woefully dissatisfied. He even went down to the bowels of the ship to complain about this peon to whatever manager he could find.

Returning to the present, Tyler replied, "Uh, yes. There was an ongoing communications problem in my quarters… This man assisted me with it."

"Did you ever see this man enter the engine compartment while you were onboard the Pescha?" the scowling man next to Cathcart asked, narrowing his eyes sharply. With that piercing gaze, Tyler couldn't help feeling *he* was being interrogated.

"I… can't say that I have, no… sir," Tyler responded. There were no clear insignias on the man's uniform, but he erred on the side of caution. The intense man felt like someone of superior rank, or at least the kind of man who made others feel that way toward him.

The man nodded over to Cathcart, and Tyler's supervisor in turn nodded back and then turned and spoke to Tyler. "Very good. That will be all, Lieutenant."

"This man…" Tyler spoke up. "He… saved my life."

The man in the cell looked up inquisitively. Cathcart raised an eyebrow. And the scowling man next to him furrowed his own brow.

"Really?" Cathcart replied, "You never mentioned that in your initial report. What did he do exactly?"

Tyler's heart raced at the question. His remark was something he blurted out without a good deal of thought. It was something that came to him almost unconsciously, instinctively. It felt true, although it would be difficult to articulate how precisely. The emergency kit was helpful, and he appreciated the gesture at the time of course, but he would have survived without it. But then, strangely enough, how would his first meeting with Anne had gone were it not for the polyscan? Perhaps he would have submitted to confinement from the start. But perhaps not. Without that level of trust being established, who knows? A hole through his torso from a plasma pistol discharge, maybe? Or, yet worse, one through Anne… He shuddered at the thought.

"I… he… it was after the crash. After I had initiated the veil. In the wreckage he provided me with a polyscan and an emergency kit and gave me some direction… to help get out of the ship. He stayed behind, while I got out."

"I see…" Cathcart remarked.

"If I may ask, sir, what charges is this man facing?"

Cathcart glanced to the man beside him, and the man spoke up. "High treason."

"Treason… sir?" Tyler asked the man.

"This traitor was intercepted several weeks ago in clandestine communication with a military vessel of the Interstellar Confederation."

"Bullshit!" the man in the cell spoke up. "I work in communications. We have to do relay pings and hails to all kinds of vessels!"

"Ha! It was no 'relay ping.' And we have evidence of other suspicious activity, but I will say no more."

"Ahem, yes," Cathcart remarked, "it is an ongoing investigation to be sure… In the meantime, did you have anything else to add, Lieutenant?"

"No… no, sir."

"Well, then, thank you again. You are free to go. Oh, and I hear you're expected to return on duty the start of next week. Is that right?"

"Yes, sir."

"Very good. Looking forward to it. Thank you, Lieutenant. You are dismissed."

"Thank you, sir."

When Tyler got back to his crew quarters, the mix of emotions was overwhelming. Seeing the old man again. It was strangely like seeing *his* old man again. As gruff and rude as he was, his was the first voice he encountered in his past life. The past life he was quickly absorbing into himself.

And the strange thing was he never even knew the man's name this whole time. Why did he think it started with a "B?" That's when it clicked. William. Bill. Of course.

But then he thought of another word starting with "B." Bridge. This man presented an opportunity. If he had any chance of fulfilling the burgeoning desire he had—if there was any way he could see a tentative aspiration come to fruition—this man could be it. He would need help. A man with technical expertise who also had every incentive to get off the ship? That would be an ally indeed. A man who could help him. A man who could help him… escape.

A WAKENING the fifth day felt like a new beginning. Tyler had purpose and direction now. He had a prepackaged breakfast sent over the vacuum tube and ate it while studying at his workstation. Ship logs. Infrastructure schematics. Ship Plan-of-the-Day. Once he was done eating, he dropped into neuro.

The rest of the morning he spent in combat simulations. Hand-to-hand. Grappling. Firearms training. Even ballistics at one point. After several hours, he decided to take a break.

That break took the form of a flying simulation. It took him a quarter-hour tweaking configurations to get it right. He had spent several years in neuro, but he had never thought to use it for flying. In retrospect, it seemed so obvious, so natural, that he had to laugh at himself for never thinking of it before.

Gliding between clouds mid-flight, a notification appeared before his eyes. Someone had entered his simulation.

The text read "Lt. Branch." With a sigh, Tyler circled back around and landed near the simulation spawn point.

"Hey, how's it going?" Tyler asked.

"I saw your environment node was open, so I figured I'd pop in," Josh replied.

"Oh… right…" Tyler replied with sudden embarrassment. In truth, he was mostly just glad Josh hadn't popped in while he was in the middle of combat training earlier. He had no wish to arouse any suspicions.

"If you wanted to be alone, I could go…"

"No, no, that's all right. Feel free to have a look around."

"What… is this place exactly?"

"It's just for flying around. Like this…" Tyler explained. And with that he hopped up and hovered a bit.

"Heh… interesting… I guess. How'd you come across this sim?"

"Oh, it's just something I built out in a few minutes. I'm thinking of playing a bit more with the muscle reflex parameters. Why don't you give it a try?"

"That's okay. I was… really just popping in." Josh's words were casual, but his furrowed brow and searching eyes betrayed otherwise. He seemed confused and strangely concerned.

"Alright. Well, if you want to meet up at the mess hall, I'll drop out in a few and head that way."

"Right… yeah, yeah, that was the other thing. Okay, yeah…"

"See you then, then."

"See you then…"

Josh took one last concerned look around before disappearing. When he did, Tyler felt a sudden mix of sorrow and pity. He couldn't see Josh understanding. At least not any time soon. Maybe not ever. He was a good man. He had his flaws like everyone else, but he generally meant well. The thought of leaving him behind was painful… but it likely would prove to be a painful necessity.

At the mess hall, there was a banquet table set out. All manner of assorted dishes atop a purple table cloth. Along the far wall were an assortment of tin cans discretely stacked, but still remaining. A visible reminder of the ultimate source of the food cooked in the walled off kitchen beyond.

The table, as it turned out, was set in honor of Commander Cathcart's birthday. Tyler remarked, "Oh, right, I completely forgot," but the more accurate truth was really that he never bothered to remember.

"This is quite a feast, eh?" Josh asked as they stood side by side waiting at the banquet table. "It looks like just about any dish you could ask for."

"Nipponese curry…" Tyler quietly voiced to himself.

"Eh, what's that?"

"What? Oh… it's, uh—it's a curry dish. These kind of potato patties and curry… yeah…"

"Huh. You said Nipponese? I thought curry was some kind of Sindhican food."

"Well, the salad looks good," Tyler said, brushing Josh's remark aside. His own remark was met with a shrug.

After Josh and Tyler ate together, shared a bit of light conversation, and parted ways, Tyler headed to the ship's gym. A neglected, quiet little room that was almost entirely empty. He vigorously worked his muscles, preparing his body just as he had prepared his mind. If there was one thing he desperately needed now, it was preparation.

THE sixth day started with soreness. His neck and lower back were aching as he rose. He splashed some warm water on his face in the little sink in his quarters and slowly dressed. He hadn't exercised that strenuously in a while. His limbs felt like they were on fire.

When Tyler got back near his desk, a soft chime sounded. It was an alert, reminding him about today's appointment in the afternoon with Healing Hands. He decided to take a light jog before and on the way to breakfast. As he was running through the halls, he bumped into Josh. Almost literally, in fact, as his old friend appeared from around a corner.

"Whoa… hey, Chris."

"Hey Josh," Tyler replied as he stopped to catch his breath.

"You, uh… heh, taking a jog?"

"Yeah… yeah. Got time to join me?"

"Not really, heh. I went into Signals to get away from that."

Tyler nodded and looked off wistfully for a moment. He had met Josh all the way back in basic. Josh went into Signals before he did, as Tyler served a brief six-month stint in the field. When they met back up with the same assignment, it was like a bit of serendipity. With a quiet sigh, Tyler turned his eyes back to Josh and spoke.

"Well, I'm pretty much done. Just going to catch some breakfast if you wanted to join me."

"Okay, sure."

After they sat down to eat, there was a moment of quiet, finally broken by Josh.

"You seem… different, these days."

"Oh?" Tyler asked with a slight gulp he tried to hide. "How so?"

"I don't know… just… I don't know."

Tyler waited a moment before carefully replying. He tried to keep things light. Keep his voice casual. "No, really man, what is it? I'm still me, heh."

Josh nodded contemplatively with a furrowed brow, gazing off into the distance, before finally speaking up. "What were you talking about the other day? All that stuff about… perpetual fighting?"

"Oh, well… I'm just… Well, to be honest, I've been feeling a little down." He knew if he told as much of the truth as he could, it would be easier to dissuade his friend.

But his friend was not so easily fooled. He looked in Tyler's eyes, then darted his own side to side. "Right… okay…"

"And, uh… I've been trying to make sense of things, y'know? I experienced some things down on Solus 4. Met some people. They weren't exactly what I was expecting."

"What do you mean…?"

"Well, obviously they were outsiders. I don't know… I guess it's hard to explain."

"And that makes you… *depressed*?"

At this point, Tyler was starting to feel interrogated. And to some extent, he may have been. Josh was searching his face with subtle intensity.

"Emotions don't have to have a rational foundation, do they? All feelings are equally valid. It's only what we do with them that merits any accountability."

Josh narrowed his eyes. And that's when Tyler knew he had perhaps stepped out of line. Those were mostly Ed's words, and he had instinctively recalled them. A half remembered rant on emotional invalidation. It wasn't exactly controversial thoughts, but Josh knew him well enough to recognize the difference. Tyler had no real interest in a number of subjects, psychology being one neglected course of study in particular.

Josh suddenly became pointed now. "Do you… *miss*… these people?"

If only I could tell him the whole truth. But he wouldn't understand. I must only tell him enough to lie.

"Well, in truth… a part of me perhaps, yeah. It's been confusing."

"Wow, I bet… Well, you're home now, man. You're like a brother to me. I hope you remember that."

"I… do. Of course, I do."

Josh seemed satisfied. But then was that his own little rouse? If it was, it was convincing. And in either case, there was nothing more to be done. Josh changed the subject and his tone, and they ate the rest of breakfast in relative peace before parting ways.

When Tyler visited Healing Hands for his checkup, his mind shifted into a state of hyper-awareness. As soon as the door slid open, he was critically analyzing the space. Scoping out its dimensions. Taking in and breaking down its nooks and crannies. He noted every detail of its interior. Counted his steps as he entered.

The medic had to repeat himself as he instructed Tyler to enter his head into the scanning apparatus. Once the scan was complete, Tyler watched the man carefully wash his hands in the copper sink. He took note of the pharmacy door nearby. Carefully observed how another medic unlocked the door with a retinal scan.

"So, everything looks great. I'm going to recommend you for duty next week just like we discussed."

The medic's remark was met with silence as Tyler continued scanning the room.

"Does that sound good to you…?" the man asked.

"What? Oh, yes. Yes. Very good. Thank you."

"Alright, well… have a good day then, Lieutenant."

"Thanks, you too."

With that the medic took a step and shrugged before carrying on. Tyler in turn walked out the door and briskly made his way back to his quarters. Tomorrow would require preparations. Final preparations.

SEVENTH day. Traditionally the day of rest. But there was no rest for Tyler. He had no time for rest. He had spent the night prior fervently working out his plan, and gathering whatever data he could. He had to be prepared for every contingency.

One question he needed to answer specifically was concerning mass. The body mass of three men in particular. At first, he had thought of medical records. But they would be inaccessible to anyone but medical personnel. Even in the Dominion with all its prying into the personal affairs of its subjects, patient privacy was still protected.

He finally had an epiphany. He could access the graviton array calibration logs. He had discovered a year ago how a maintenance portal on the ship's intranet had been made accessible with plain text authentication. He had thought to report it back then, but usually such reports went unaddressed for long periods of time, and if there were any incidents he would be the first suspected. Accordingly, he stayed silent. Now, he was glad he had. When he checked the night prior, he discovered the plain text authentication was still in place. He had only to sniff for packets and wait.

And so he did, and in the morning he discovered he had what he needed. Credentials into the maintenance logs. From there, he ran the data through a mass displacement calculation routine he had scripted together.

Once done, he had his answer. 80, 86, and 88 kilograms each. At a dose rate of 13 milligrams per kilogram, that would be between 1,040 and 1,144 mg in order to effect a result of approximately 25 minutes. That would probably be enough time. Probably…

The weight of what he was about to do pulled him down. It gave him a sinking feeling in his gut. His feet felt even heavier than usual in that artificial gravity, as he stood with his eyes closed in quiet meditation. But there was no time like the present. It was now or never. And so he strode out the door.

"Lieutenant Tyler. Back so soon?" the medic asked when he came through the door to Healing Hands.

"Heh, yeah. I'm getting some kind of stomach ache."

"Oh really?"

"It doesn't feel too serious. Do you think I could get some antacid or something maybe?"

"Yeah, sure thing. Have a seat."

Tyler feigned to sit, but as soon as the man walked to the recessed alcove where the pharmacy door was, he crept behind. Once he was at the door, suitably out of sight, Tyler grabbed him from behind in a chokehold.

"G-gah!" the man exclaimed with a raspy gasp as Tyler squeezed the man's throat with his forearm.

"I'm sorry about this…" he whispered to the man as he finally went limp.

Tyler quickly propped the man's head up, and held the lids of an unconscious eye open to the retinal scanner. He rushed into the pharmaceutical closet and quickly searched for ketamine. He would only have a few seconds.

Injectable drugs. Arranged alphabetically. He reminded himself of the system and quickly found several vials. By the time he was done calibrating the injector gun, the passed out man was starting to groan.

Tyler rushed over to the man, brought the gun to his neck, and pulled the trigger. As soon as he did, he started counting down in his head. *59, 58, 57…* He would need to administer it over the course of a minute to be safe. The last thing he wanted weighing on his conscience was anyone's death if he could possibly avoid it. He dragged the man into the closet as he progressively administered the drug.

Next stop: Brig.

"Can I help you, sir?" the first of the two guards asked as Tyler entered the door of the brig. The man stepped away from his station to meet Tyler.

"I received a notification from Commander Cathcart. Is he not here?"

"No, sir."

"Strange. It could have been an old notification from the other day. I've been having issues with ship communications lately, heh. Just to be sure, could you double-check he didn't send out a notice. He could be expecting to meet me here."

"Uh, sure thing, sir."

As the man turned and walked a pace or two back toward his desk, Tyler quickly grabbed him from behind.

"Stay where you are! Hands up!" Tyler shouted out to the other guard. He quickly undid the strap and pulled out the first guard's plasma pistol with his right hand as he choked the man's neck with his left arm.

Once the other man put up his hands, Tyler barked again, "Now back away from the desk!"

The guard slowly backed away from the desk as the first guard went limp. Tyler kept his pistol trained on the second guard as he carefully pulled out the injector gun with his left hand and administered ketamine to the first guard.

"You're not going to get away with this!"

Tyler ignored the man's excited remark, and simply stared, making sure not to break eye contact.

"Your turn," Tyler stated coldly.

"Fuck no!"

"Would you prefer I choke hold you first?"

"You fucking sovedamn traitor!"

"You should watch your language. This is a Kyrian vessel," Tyler remarked wryly as he gestured for the man to turn around.

He injected the man in the back of the neck while he kept his pistol squarely aimed with the other hand. The man's raised arms slowly lowered as his knees buckled. Tyler grabbed the man, carefully lowering him to the ground, and continued to administer the drug over the course of a minute as the man went completely limp.

"If I let you out, I'm assuming you'll help me?" Tyler asked, as he started to undress one of the guards. His heart raced as the man in the cell eyed him incredulously.

"Help you… do what exactly?"

"Escape. This ship is leaving orbit tonight."

The man tilted his head side to side, examining Tyler, as Tyler quickly pulled the guard's jumpsuit over his own. The man started to chuckle. "Heh, yeah, alright… yeah, shit, what do I have to lose?"

Tyler released the door locks. As soon as the door started to slide open, he called out, "Alright, let's go! Let's go!"

"What's the plan?"

"We're going to put these on behind your back," Tyler ordered as he grabbed a pair of restraints.

"Shit, seriously?"

"You think anyone's just going to let you stroll out of here without an escort?"

The grizzled man turned around with a sigh.

The two briskly marched through the corridors of the ship without much notice. Brig guards weren't well known to most other departments. To be safe, however, Tyler planned to avoid people as much as possible. In that regard, he discretely led his prisoner to the service stairway.

"Aw man, are we seriously taking the steps?"

"We need to minimize our chances of exposure. I don't work in the brig."

"Just where do you work, Johnny?" the man asked with a chuckle as they started to ascend the steps.

"Why in the world do you keep calling me that anyways?" Tyler asked with a moderate amount of irritation.

"Heh, it's your name, isn't it? Jon-ah C. Tyler, right?"

"Seriously?" Tyler asked in a shock, leaving him dead in his tracks. "It's *Jonah*. And didn't I introduce myself as Chris?"

"Yeah, yeah. Just giving you grief, man. You sure as hell gave me enough of that."

Tyler went silent, and continued his ascent. Left step. Sigh. Right step. "I'm… sorry for all that. I'm ashamed of how I acted. I don't want to be that… person."

This in turn led the old man to stop in his tracks. He peered back at Tyler before nodding his head and continuing. "Alright… name's Bill, by the way."

"I… remember."

After several flights of stairs and a fair amount of huffing —Bill wasn't in the best of shape—they finally reached the floor Tyler wanted. Flight deck.

"Here," Tyler said as he gestured for Bill to turn around. "We're going to switch things up. Now you're the guard, and I'm… heh… me."

Bill was glad to get the restraints off. "If this was the plan, you could have removed these as soon as we got in here."

"Just had to give you one last bit of grief, eh?" Tyler remarked with a smirk.

After Bill was dressed in the guard's uniform, and Jonah was back in his own, they quietly emerged out onto the deck and made their way to the hangar bay door. The small hangar didn't have a lot of men manning it. The Selenium after all was primarily a surveillance ship. It had a handful of small form craft for reconnaissance scouting and that was about it.

Nevertheless, they would still need a distraction. For that, Tyler came prepared. He gestured Bill to follow him a few paces back from the door. From a deep pocket he pulled out a small book. His old personal copy of the Libben.

"Please don't tell me the next part of the plan involves devotional reading."

"Heh, not quite. Stand back…"

Tyler adjusted the phase dial on his plasma pistol and carefully aimed it so the beam would scurry along the surface of the book, carefully catching it on fire without incinerating it all at once.

"That should do it…"

In less than half a minute, the fire alarm sounded, and the corridor started to fill with foam. A few minutes later, a couple of men rushed out a door to one side of the hangar. Tyler noted which one and gestured for Bill to follow him to the other door on the other side. There they waited for another half minute as another man—one who should be the last one, per Tyler's reckoning—made his way out of the door to investigate.

Tyler and Bill entered the hangar discretely, and briskly started heading towards one of the crafts. They made it past to the front of the fuselage of one craft, the side facing away from the rest of the bay out toward the bay doors. As they did, a man stepped out from between the crafts. A man brandishing a pistol. A man Tyler immediately recognized.

"Josh…"

"Damn it, Chris!" Josh exclaimed in furor. "I was seriously hoping I was wrong…"

"I'm sorry, Josh, but *I'm* hoping I don't have to use *this*," Tyler replied, pointing with his eyes at the pistol in his own hand.

"You're going to shoot me now?"

"Well, what were you planning on doing with *that*?"

"Damn it, Chris! The One damn it all to hell! What are you thinking?!"

"Thinking? For the first time in a while, I feel like I *am* thinking. I'm thinking more clearly than ever."

"Don't be a fool! Where are you going to go? Down to that planet? Down to those degenerates?" At this point, Josh caught sight of Bill standing off to one side. "And who the hell is this? Fuck!"

"I'm going to need help to escape."

"Escape?! What the fuck are you talking about? Escape? You mean from your duty? I can't believe this!"

"I can't believe a number of things myself anymore, Josh."

"They—they did this to you, didn't they? You're *not* thinking clearly, man. They have you strapped to a silver chair. Pure delusion!"

"If there's any silver chair, it's this ship and everything it represents. And I mean to get out."

"I'm *not* going to let you throw your life away!"

"Whoever wishes to gain his life must lose it…"

"I… I don't even know what to say."

"Say you'll let us go. There's still time for you to sneak out of here and go back if that's what you want."

"If that's what I want? You think I'd want to go with *you?*"

"You would be more than welcome if you did."

Josh scowled and ground his teeth. They remained at an impasse with both pistols drawn on one another. *Whoever wishes to gain his life must lose it.* Those words echoed in Tyler's head, and he realized what he had to do.

"If you won't let me live as I will…" Tyler stated, before slowly lowering his pistol. "Then you might as well kill me now. I won't be a part of this anymore."

"Are you calling my bluff?"

"Let's call it a matter of faith."

"Damn it, Chris! We can still go back! You—you can say you weren't in your right mind! I know you've been through a lot!"

"I can't go back. I won't go back. So you're going to have to either get out of my way… or kill me."

Josh's eyes danced back and forth in Tyler's. Tyler in turn gazed at his friend in resigned love. If he had to be killed by anyone, it might as well be Josh. Any fear he felt by the prospect was displaced by pity. If only he had more time, perhaps… but how much time? Weeks? Months? Years? A lifetime could pass, and he might never convince his friend to see the world as he now did.

If it had to end this way, at least he could die knowing his friend felt he was doing the right thing just as much as he did. And if there was to be any hope of living, he could not bring himself to offset his chances by shooting his friend—assuming he could even do as much unscathed. He could only hold out hope that by setting the example of submitting to death, he could demonstrate how much this meant. He could hope that Josh would take his gesture of peace and maybe—just maybe—return the gesture in kind.

Time stood still for a long moment. Tyler focused on his breath. Closed his eyes in peace. Extended his hands out, showing his palms and bearing his chest like an open target. He listened to his heart. Waited for whatever might come next.

And then it finally happened. Josh sighed. As Tyler opened his eyes, he could see his friend had lowered his weapon.

"Fine. Have it your way, Chris. Get out of here. I never saw you."

Tyler nodded somberly and breathed a sigh of relief. He was going to sorely miss Josh. After a brief moment of a long gaze to the side, Tyler spoke up. "If we meet again, my friend… call me Jonah."

Josh looked to the side and shook his head.

"Just go before I change my mind."

Josh left quietly as the two men entered the small craft they would use to make their escape. One of those two men felt like a new man. Snatched from the jaws of death. And yet, in accepting that fate, it was as though he died. To die and be born anew. And with that new birth, he remembered the child within. The name from his childhood. The name from his mother. From now on, he would be someone he had once known and forgotten. That same someone he had rediscovered when he had forgotten. Jonah.

"Well, that was intense, eh?" Bill remarked.

Jonah whiffed out a small laugh and smirked at Bill's vulgar observation. The incongruity of its understatement seemed fitting to the little he knew of Bill's peculiar personality. Even as he had rediscovered himself, Jonah was discovering that he was really starting to like his gruff older companion—or at least find him strangely entertaining.

Jonah entered his emergency authorization clearance codes to open the bay doors. His treason would have little question now. His authorization would be on the record. But it didn't matter anymore. One driving thought overruled all others. *I'm coming home, Anne.*

JONAH and Bill sped away from the hangar with little issue. They flew past the magnetic containment field beyond the bay doors, out into a sea of stars. Whether it was the view beyond, the shift to the locally calibrated graviton array onboard the ship, or a mixture of both, Jonah felt like a weight had been lifted. Peace and calm washed over him as he looked out to those stars.

Jonah's heart then beat with excitement as the shuttle craft circled around the Selenium and Solus 4 came into view. The blue-green marble shone in the dark like a precious gem, glittering in the light of a distant sun. What glory in the heavens could compare with the beauty of such a world?

He didn't have long to marvel, however, before the com panel lit up. The Selenium was hailing them. Jonah took a long breath before accepting the connection request.

"Shuttle Juliet Oscar November Two One Zero this is the DSS Selenium flight deck requesting justification for emergency departure," a monotone voice rattled off rapidly.

"DSS Selenium, Shuttle ending Two One Zero responding, Lieutenant Tyler speaking. Justification Bravo Mike independent military threat assessment, communique waiver authorization Commander Cathcart."

Approximately ten seconds passed before they received a response from another voice. "Tyler, this is Commander Cathcart. What the hell is going on?"

"Greetings, Commander Cathcart, sir. As I detailed in my briefing communication, this matter was too urgent not to merit immediate action. I am en route to investigate and potentially confirm accordingly, sir."

"What communication? What are you talking about?"

"The briefing report I sent prior to departure, sir. Did you not receive it, sir?"

"No! And this is highly irregular. What could possibly merit a departure in this sector? You haven't even been admitted to duty!"

"The reactor at Talos Mystico, sir. I have reason to believe the station may be using it to construct plasma weapons or even a fusion bomb. As I outlined in my report—"

"What are you blathering on about, lieutenant? There is nothing of strategic interest in this entire stellar—what? When? The brig?"

The channel went mute. Jonah let out a sigh.

"Lock in your safety harness. I'm shutting off the graviton array and taking us to four G's."

Bill nodded and strapped his harness as Jonah disabled the array. There was a momentary sensation of weightlessness, before Jonah slammed the throttle forward, sinking them into their seats. In a minute, they had gone from 100 to over 8,000 kph.

Two minutes or so passed before they were hailed again…

"Lieutenant Tyler, this is your captain speaking. Turn the craft around *immediately*!"

"Sir, this reconnaissance is of paramount importance!" Jonah shouted in a rumbling, raspy voice, struggling to breathe with his lungs compressed as the craft continued to speed along. "We need confirmation on the—"

"Lieutenant, you are way out of line! Telemetry has determined from your propulsion trail the adjusted mass of the shuttle. We know you are harboring a fugitive. I repeat, turn your craft around NOW!"

Jonah strained under the acceleration to mute the channel. He shifted his eyes to Bill without turning his head and said, "On my mark, prepare to dump the liquid helium lines."

"What? Why?!" Bill called out in the midst of the rumbling fury of the speeding ship.

"If they decide to blow us out of the sky, it's the only real defense we have!"

"Shit!"

"On my second mark, prepare to shut down all ship systems."

"Shit, shit, shit!"

"Understand?!"

"Yes! Okay! Got it!"

Another voice came on the channel. A voice Jonah recognized with dread and a bit of loathing. A cold baritone voice filled with condescension…

"Brother Tyler… This is Rector Falwell. It is not too late to turn around. The Sovereign's love can cover over a multitude of transgressions."

Jonah saved his breath and stayed silent as a lamb.

"Brother Tyler…? If I cannot urge you to repentance, then I am afraid I must hand you over to the higher authorities in this matter…"

After a moment of silence, the captain returned to the call. "Your continued defiance will not be tolerated. Turn your shuttle around and surrender yourself and the fugitive into custody, or I *will* open fire…"

Jonah answered him nothing.

"Once the shuttle reaches the 50 kilometer mark, launch a plasma torpedo," the man said as an aside to another. Then returning to address Jonah, he said, "Final warning, Lieutenant!"

Jonah cut the channel and called out to Bill. "Ready with the helium?!"

"It's ready!"

Jonah watched on the rear sensor display as the plasma torpedo shot out of the ship like a flaming burst of dragon's breath. It rapidly made its way toward their position on the display grid as he waited in silence.

"NOW!"

The liquid helium drained from the veins of the small craft, bursting out behind them like a cloud of clear blood.

"Mark two! Shutdown all systems now!"

Only a second after the lights went out when Bill killed all power to the shuttle, the craft was rocked with an explosion. The shockwave of the plasma torpedo impacting the cloud of liquid helium. They were saved.

Jonah blew out a large breath before turning to Bill. "We made it through the flames, but we're not out of the kitchen yet."

Over the course of a quarter-hour, Jonah explained to his companion the plan and what they were up against at this point. He figured they had a good chance of being considered dead. And they would need that cover of death in order to live.

In that regard, they would need to keep all ship systems at an absolute minimum. That meant no power of any kind for the next three hours. Considering the interior of the craft was approximately one hundred cubic meters, they could survive that long without much issue. But at around the three-hour point, they would need to enable the oxygen pumps to keep from suffocating.

They were traveling at over 50,000 kph at this point. Their entire remaining trip would take them a little over seven hours. Once they reached the atmosphere of the planet, they would then have the additional challenge of making it through without burning up on entry.

Close to an hour passed in silence. Dread and anxiety over their current predicament sat in the shuttle like a fog of despair. The lingering menace of the Selenium somewhere out in space made them mute. When they did start to talk, it was in hushed tones, as though by being quiet they could help to avoid detection.

"So… how did you manage to survive? Back on the Pescha, that is. The waterfall."

"Heh…" Bill whispered his reply. "I inverted the graviton array."

"You did what?"

"The graviton array. I inverted it. Well, specifically I calibrated it to project a gravitational field at a perpendicular alignment, directly counter to the gravity of the planet. I managed to tap in to the array controls while you were out scanning the ship."

"Wow, that's… pretty clever."

Bill shrugged. "It worked well enough. Just had to time it right."

"Huh…"

Jonah was strangely impressed. He was starting to gain the awareness that there was more to Bill than met the eye. How many telecommunications technicians would know how to re-calibrate a graviton array? And how many would have thought to do it in that particular situation?

"What then? How did you get out of the ship?"

"Well, first I had to cut my legs loose. They weren't doing me any good."

Jonah winced at the thought of it.

"After that quick work with a hacksaw I found in a cabinet, I pulled myself around to the ladder—which was more of a bridge at that point. Took me a while, but I managed to crawl on out of the ship, climb down a rope, and splashed in the river.

"I figured if I was gonna die, might as well get some fresh air before I did, eh?"

At that, Bill and Jonah laughed vigorously. Intense laughter born mostly out of nerves that they both tried to stifle in that dark quiet interior.

"Anyhow," Bill continued, "I laid out on that shore for a day or two before they came and picked me up."

A couple more hours passed. The air inside the cabin was exceedingly close and uncomfortably warm. They were both starting to suffer from dizziness and headaches. Droplets of sweat drifted about the cabin, floating in its weightless environment.

"I think it's about time we turned on the air," Jonah finally stated.

"Yes. *Please.*"

After disengaging the craft's system from standby, Jonah did a quick systems check. Everything seemed to be in decent working condition, until he noticed one system in particular…

"Damn it…" Jonah remarked.

"What is it?"

"Looks like our reverse thrusters are offline. Probably damaged by the EM pulse of the blast."

"But I shut everything down…"

"Latent internal capacitors. Or something tripped up in the power grid. I was expecting our imaging network to be out, but not this. Damn it…"

"So where does that put us?"

"It puts us in not such a great spot. Our atmospheric entry is going to be… complicated."

"Shit… Turn and burn, eh?" Bill asked casually.

"I'm not sure if our thermal panels will take it."

"It'll be a hot ride, but I think we can make it. Landing might be a killer, heh…"

Jonah whiffed a small laugh at Bill's dark remark. The irony of making it all the way through one incineration, only to face another. Or to make it through both and finally be torn apart on the planet's surface.

"Wait a minute…" Jonah said with furrowed brow and darting eyes. "What about your graviton trick?"

"We're calling it a trick now?"

"Heh, how about *maneuver*?"

"I like it. The Bill Maneuver."

Jonah nodded and smiled with hope, before Bill continued.

"But there's a big difference between a few hundred-meter drop of a big freighter ship and a several hundred kph crash landing of a shuttle like this. The Bill Maneuver only works when you have an array intact enough to make it work."

"What if we extended the field effect beyond the craft? Cushion the whole thing against itself."

"Hmm…" Bill mused. "Maybe… I doubt we'd have enough power to do it for very long at all. Just a matter of seconds really at this point. But, hell, what else we got?"

Jonah nodded, before furrowing his brow again. "What else, indeed… Perhaps I could talk to the station early, let them know what we're facing and ask for help."

"And risk those bastards intercepting our communication?"

"Is there some way we could fly under the radar? Or the radio in this case, I guess."

"Well… you could do single band localized one-way transmission. That would help. They wouldn't be able to easily get a position on its source that way. But they'd still know what was said."

"Unless it was encrypted…"

"Alright… alright. But you'd still have to get them a key. A passphrase or something. Assuming you want them to *de*-crypt your message."

"I have an idea for that…"

Close to half an hour passed as Jonah sat and slowly typed and re-typed something on the console near his seat. Bill leaned over his shoulder and caught a glimpse of what he was doing and laughed.

"Out here close to death, and you're writing poetry?"

"Is there a more appropriate time for poetry?"

"Spoken like a poet."

Jonah chuckled and shook his head. "It's a riddle. One where the answer is only really deducible by a targeted party. One of the oldest forms of cryptography, really."

"'Speak "friend" and enter,'⁵ eh?"

"Heh, something like that…"

SEVERAL hours had passed before Jonah finally transmitted his communication to the station. Part of it encrypted. Part of it not. And all of it along a single-band localized one-way transmission with Bill's help.

The blue-green marble progressively grew larger. And with it, their tension. With their imaging sensor network out and no reverse thrust, they would have to get their entry trajectory just right. Too shallow and they would bounce out. Too deep and they might just burn up. At over 50,000 kph, the margin for error was extremely narrow.

A tense silence lingered in the cabin as they made their approach. They circled around the planet, beginning their descent maneuver in the dark of late twilight before dusk. The darkness burned away, filled with flame as they tore through the upper atmosphere.

The craft rattled and rumbled along as they streaked across the sky in a mad dash around the planet's circumference. Sweat dripped from their silent furrowed brows, falling in the same direction they were now. Falling and falling, but slower and slower as they went.

The flames subsided and Jonah began a series of s-turns as they glided swiftly closer and closer to the ground. As they soared through and around the air, they could start to make out shadowy shapes below in the predawn twilight. A snaking river between trees. Hills and mountains below wisps of clouds.

It was all so beautiful. Jonah now could only hope that they would survive the landing long enough to enjoy it. Had anyone received their message? And if they had, had they been able to decipher his riddle and deduce the decryption key? If they had, he specifically made it clear not to respond until their arrival at this approximate time.

As they banked closer and closer, Jonah could make out something below. It was flying, but looked too big to be a bird. Could it be…?

A ping lit up on the com panel. Jonah rushed to answer it immediately.

"Hey, pal, you there?"

"Frank!" Jonah exclaimed excitedly.

"Is that you, Jonah?"

"Yes! It's me, Frank! It's so good to hear your voice."

"You never told me you could pilot a shuttle, buddy!"

"Well, here I am!" Jonah said with a laugh and a tear in his eye. "Now let's just hope I can land this thing, eh?"

"We've rolled out the red carpet down here for you. Well, not literally. A carpet won't do you as much good. We have a big elastic net and some magnetic field generators. Got the other three 'ropters holding it all in place."

"You're a literal lifesaver, man! I'm going to try and shoot for a water landing. I think I can bank it in to this river here."

"Sounds good. Just don't fall off the edge. If you're looking where I think you're looking, that's Wellington Falls."

"Ha, sure thing!" Jonah laughed, letting out some nervous energy. "I'm opening up a data channel. I can transmit you a feed of my course and trajectory as it changes."

"Sounds good. We're tracking you down here. Just bring her in nice and easy."

The craft swooped around lower and lower as Jonah continued to bank back and forth, slowing as he went. Finally, they were on their final approach, flying right above a sea of trees before centering between them, racing along the river between the blur of green to either side.

"Bill Maneuver, now!"

Bill nodded excitedly and slammed his finger down on his panel, engaging the array inversion routine. For two to three seconds, they violently lurched forward as the craft was pulled back by a gravitational field from the aft side. It acted as a kind of invisible parachute, slowing them down as they glided just above the broad stream. The effect then disengaged, and they touched down on the water. The craft skidded along the surface, skipping like a rock over the river.

As they slowed down along that liquid runway, they finally came to a relative stop a hundred meters or so away from the river's edge at the cataract. There like a fence floating in the air at the edge was a large net suspended by two hyperopters, and held in place by a third unseen craft hovering below the drop.

A fourth hyperopter circled around above, before descending to their position.

"Awesome landing!" Frank shouted over the com channel with a laugh in his voice. "I guess you didn't need our help after all, eh?"

"Haha, I'm so glad you're here, man!" Jonah replied. "Do you think we could hitch a ride before we sink?"

"Alright, but it ain't cheap. You owe me one."

"Can I make you a sandwich when we get back?"

"Deal."

Jonah and Bill emerged through the emergency hatch on the top of the craft. From there, they took Frank's hand and stepped out on to the hovering ramp extended below the hyperopter. As they entered the cabin, Jonah greeted Sumi, who was piloting the craft, and briefly introduced Bill to them both.

They flew a short distance over the forest for several minutes, making their way to a distant lake. *The* lake. Those crystal shores where Jonah had first met the love of his life. Back then, a short life. But then what life isn't?

The four hyperopters landed together into a great circle from four different directions. In addition to Frank and Sumi of course, there stepped out from the other crafts Dr. Jenkins and a nurse assistant, the station director, one or two others Jonah hadn't recognized, Dr. Reed, and finally—with a leap of his heart—Anne.

As Jenkins and her assistant immediately began checking on Jonah and Bill, most everyone else stood about with cautious smiles. He could see in their eyes a touch of hesitance. Was this truly the same man that had been taken from them a week ago? He looked much the same, save the uniform. Several eyed the rank insignia on his chest and glanced over him in cautious curiosity.

"I'm… I'm back, everyone."

"Welcome back," Anne said with a hopeful warmth.

"I guess it goes without saying I wish to defect," Jonah remarked.

His statement was met with nervous laughter. Jonah scratched the back of his neck out of his own nerves. Here he was back at the lake, wondering what he would have to do to regain everyone's trust.

"I can vouch for this man," Bill spoke up. "He saved my life… and risked his own to do so."

"Excuse me. I'm Doctor Ericson, the director of this station. Who are you again?" the station director asked pointedly. Hearing the director's name made Jonah think of his brother, and in turn his mother. Staring off into the golden light of morning, his heart was moved at the prospect of seeing them again. In the meantime, Bill turned to Ericson and replied…

"William Evans… ICSA. Your military escort can verify my identity via genomic analysis when they arrive tomorrow."

"I can vouch for you right now, Special Agent Evans," Sumi spoke up. Her remark was met with confusion by everyone, most especially Frank. "I was briefed on your mission six months ago. Agent Kaneko, ICSA."

"Heh," Bill replied. "So you were my contact… Sorry I'm late."

Sumi turned to Frank and shook her head at his hanging jaw. "I was gonna tell you tomorrow after we left."

"Is anyone here *not* a spy?" Ed asked.

"Heh, well not me, Dr. Reed. Not anymore. I… could use a career change."

Ed nodded his head warmly and looked long into Jonah's eyes, searching out his soul. With a broad smile, he extended his arms and said, "C'mon, man, bring it in."

Ed hugged him tightly with tears in his eyes, squeezing him close like a loving father to a prodigal son.

"Heh," Jonah said as they ended their embrace. "We have a *lot* to talk about."

"I'm sure we do," Ed said. They both sniffed as they wiped their faces, filled as they were now with tears of long sought joy.

"I got your message," Anne said with a wide grin.

"I knew you'd figure it out," Jonah said.

"Well, in truth, I had to run it by Ed," she said with a warm chuckle.

"It was a joint effort," Ed remarked.

"What was that message again?" Bill interjected.

"Something sweet and effective," Anne replied. "Here…"

With that, she pulled out a tablet, then pulled up the message and read it aloud to Jonah's mild embarrassment...

Dearest Anne,

A dozen letters minus one,
two names reveal the setting son.
Your mother's wisdom is the key,
plus the name which you call me.

"'SophiaJonah,'" Ed said with a nod.

Jonah turned, finally stepped closer to Anne and reached out his hands to hold hers. "Anne… I… I missed you *so* much."

Anne simply nodded, wiping away her own tears now.

"I was confused, and… at war with myself. And it took me a while to see the truth. To see it more clearly than I've ever seen it before, at least. But I did see it. And that's when I knew I needed to get back."

"What was the truth you saw?"

Jonah paused for a moment, gazing off into the distance of the day's golden dawn, as he thought wistfully. And then he returned, gazing long into her eyes with wonder and joy.

"It's hard to express, but it's something like… if the

potter has power over the clay, then why would he tie two together unless that be his will?”

"I'm not sure I entirely understand," she said with a tear-filled laugh. She was really just happy to be in his presence again.

"Nor do I. But I feel at peace. A peace that transcends all understanding. If there's one thing I know now, it's this: I love you and I always will. I love you more than tongue can tell. I know no greater truth than this."

And with that they kissed and embraced. An embrace as inseparable as yin and yang. Their bodies and souls entwined in the eternal moment. The only moment in which they'd ever been or ever would be.

Different Vessels

Acknowledgments

I must thank my mother for tirelessly listening every week as I composed this "short story" which progressively became longer and larger in scope. Thanks to little Ichko for listening at nap time to a (slightly edited, sometimes summarized) version of this tale as well. Thanks to my wife and the rest of my family for patiently waiting. Waiting to share this work with someone in its entirety motivated me to see it through to completion. Special thanks to my dear brother Jason Eric Lee, after whom I have named two individuals now—including the more recent one in this work who happens to be fictional—and who has been steadily goading me into writing a novel. Here it is at last.

Cited Works

The following works contain enough nuggets of truth that it seemed fitting that they should exist in some fashion, even in the alternate world of this novel. For those remotely familiar with these works, the references in this book may seem all too obvious, but for those who may not be, I wish to highlight my indebtedness to the genius of these authors.

1   Lewis, C. S. Chapter 12. In *Out of the Silent Planet*.
2   Thomas, Dylan. *Do not go gentle into that good night*.
3   Lewis, C. S. Human Pain. In *The Problem of Pain*.
4   Lewis, C. S. Chapter 10. In *Perelandra*.
5   Tolkien, J. R. R. Chapter 4. In *The Fellowship of the Ring*.